On a long loop of ribbon, a clump of mistletoe dangled from the ceiling. He reacted instantly.

But while Mike had the honed reflexes of a fighter pilot, Merry had a head start. The cold air made his lungs seize, but he got the words out. "Don't you want…me to…kiss you?"

She frowned. "Not with my parents pushing us together so obviously. Not with you leaving in only a week. Not when we're both pressured by the circumstances."

He dropped the timbre of his voice to a conspiratorial level that was only partly joking. "What are these circumstances you speak of?"

She blinked. "You don't know?"

"Nick told me lots of things, including that you and the guy you lived with split up recently. Is that what you mean? Are you brokenhearted?"

"I'm not brokenhearted," she whispered. "But I am…"

"Eminently kissable," he said, and gathered her into his arms so she couldn't run away again. He took her mouth with certainty. After a moment he deepened the kiss and dropped his hands to her waist.

Ding. A bell went off in his head. *Plink.* The penny dropped. *Click.* Pieces came together.

"Meredith." She looked straight at him, nodding a little. "You're pregnant."

Dear Reader,

A town called Christmas actually exists. It's located near Lake Superior, on highway M-28 in the Upper Peninsula of Michigan. Giant Mr. and Mrs. Claus signs welcome visitors to the Christmas mall, while the town's post office hand-cancels Christmas cards sent from around the country. Though my version of Christmas, Michigan, has been fictionalized to include the tree farm of the heroine's family, the Parade of Lights and a tavern named the Christmas Cheer, the essence of the rugged, can-do spirit remains true to life.

I hope you find a little quiet time during your own busy holiday season to enjoy Merry and Mike's story.

Happy holidays!

Carrie

P.S. Visit my Web site at www.CarrieAlexander.com for Christmas cookie recipes and news about future Harlequin Superromance projects.

A TOWN CALLED
CHRISTMAS
Carrie Alexander

HARLEQUIN®

TORONTO • NEW YORK • LONDON
AMSTERDAM • PARIS • SYDNEY • HAMBURG
STOCKHOLM • ATHENS • TOKYO • MILAN • MADRID
PRAGUE • WARSAW • BUDAPEST • AUCKLAND

ISBN-13: 978-0-373-71455-1
ISBN-10:   0-373-71455-6

A TOWN CALLED CHRISTMAS

ABOUT THE AUTHOR

A lifelong Michigander, Carrie Alexander has been writing for more than a decade, garnering two RITA® Award nominations and a *Romantic Times BOOKreviews* career achievement award along the way. At Christmastime she indulges her artistic side by spending too many hours wrapping gifts, creating birch-bark wreaths and decorating sugar cookies.

Books by Carrie Alexander

HARLEQUIN SUPERROMANCE

Don't miss any of our special offers. Write to us at the following address for information on our newest releases.

Harlequin Reader Service
U.S.: 3010 Walden Ave., P.O. Box 1325, Buffalo, NY 14269
Canadian: P.O. Box 609, Fort Erie, Ont. L2A 5X3

To my father:
Christmas tree seller, ski jumper
and storyteller extraordinaire

PROLOGUE

LIEUTENANT COMMANDER Michael Kavanaugh relished the crucial seconds of the strike fighter's final approach to the aircraft carrier. For that brief time, he had nothing else occupying his mind. His sorry excuse for a personal life vanished. All that mattered were his years of flight experience—from the first day of ground school through combat sorties to making just one more successful trip.

He entered the traffic pattern at two hundred and fifty knots, flying up the wake of the ship with his tailhook down, and completed a brisk break turn and deceleration. Landing gear and flaps extended.

A red indicator light blinked on his instrument panel. Too fast. He pitched nose up, passing the ship's port side now. A turn to final approach, hand on throttle, looking for the "meatball," the colored-light array that was his optical landing aid. The orange meatball was centered, indicating an optimum glide slope. One clipped radio announcement and response from the landing signal officer and he was good to go.

Final approach. Every thought, every sensation, narrowed to an arrow point of concentration. The small, rapid corrections he made to maintain the ideal angle were automatic.

The plane hit the deck with a solid thump. Mike jammed full throttle in anticipation of a bolter—where the tailhook bounced past the ship's arrestor wires despite a perfect approach—but the hook caught and he was safely aboard.

He exhaled. That was it. The last "E" ticket ride of the day.

Still high on the rush, he looked to a yellow-shirted crew member for directions to taxi the Rhino to its parking spot.

Afterward, still in his green flight suit, Mike reported to his home away from home, the Blue Knight squadron's ready room. The room was outfitted with rows of assigned chairs, a television and other amenities, along with the banners and crest of the squadron. Grades for the day's approaches would be posted, but that wasn't his present focus.

He exchanged greetings with a couple of pilots before settling into his padded chair, wishing that just once there might be some privacy. It was a futile wish, but there'd been nothing else for him, lately.

With grim resolution, he reached into an inside pocket, feeling the strain where the shoulder harness had bruised his collarbone. The letter he withdrew was already familiar in his hand, even though he'd received it only a few days ago, four months in to the cruise. He had every word memorized, but then that had been an easy task. The letter was short and concise, as if Denise hadn't wanted to waste any more time or words on the breakup of their lengthy engagement.

Mike unfolded the letter. Reading it again was like prodding an aching tooth with his tongue. He did it over and over to see if it had stopped hurting.

Soon enough, it would. Because even though the news had hit him in the gut like a swallow of Applejack, Denise was right. There was no great love lost between them, only injured pride.

The letter was dated the twenty-fourth of May.

Dear Michael,

You must already know what I'm going to write. I heard it in your voice the last time we talked. We haven't really been in love for a long time now.

That doesn't mean I'm not sorry to do this. You'll take it as a failure, but you shouldn't. It's more my fault than yours. I just didn't know how lonely it would be, waiting for you to come back. Although, to be brutally honest, there were times you seemed a thousand miles away even when you were here.

What I see now is that my feelings for you aren't strong enough to take the frequent separations of military life. I doubt yours are, either.

So I can't marry you. I'm sorry.

I'll always remember you and the good times we had, but I know that this is the right thing to do. And you believe in doing the right thing, don't you? That's practically your mantra.

Maybe one day we'll meet again, in happier circumstances.

Yours truly,

Denise

CHAPTER ONE

"ARE YOU CERTAIN we're not at the North Pole?" Michael surveyed the frigid landscape beyond the ice-encrusted windows of the rental car. After his deployment to the Persian Gulf earlier that year, he was familiar with loneliness and deprivation, but he'd never been to a place as cold and isolated as this before.

The strange new world was nearly colorless. Out of the flannel sky, fat, lazy snowflakes spiraled toward the windshield in random loops and whirls. A frosty two-lane highway stretched away into a frigid forest of bare branches and ragged pines, which were burdened by mantles of heavy snow. Even the sun seemed leached of warmth and color, a tissue-paper disk hidden behind layers of clouds.

Michael shivered inside his Navy-issued topcoat. His bleak mood offered no more warmth than the rental car's faulty heater.

Christmas in a town called Christmas. The stuff of sugar plum dreams, except he wasn't buying it. There was no magic remaining in Mike's world.

"Gotta be the North Pole," he grumbled.

"Nah." Nicholas York shoved the heating lever up to full blast, hoping to eke out another degree of warmth. The hearty Yooper—a common slang term for a denizen of Michigan's Upper Peninsula—had been Mike's closest friend since flight school in Corpus Christi, right on through to their present assignment in the Blue Knight strike fighter squadron. "Not unless our pilot took a wrong turn."

Michael grunted. "I didn't like the look of the man." They'd connected in Detroit, flown north in a rinky-dink prop plane, then disembarked at an airport in the middle of nowhere. From there they'd driven over a hundred miles deeper into nowhere. Maybe they had traveled *beyond* the North Pole.

"Only because you hate giving up control," Nicky said cheerfully.

He had good reason to be cheerful. Nicky was going home for the holidays, to his wife and children. While Mike was glad their leave had come through at the last minute, for the Yorks's sake, he sure wished *he* had a better plan than extra-wheeling it with someone else's family for the holidays. If Nicky hadn't insisted, Mike might have spent the time off hunkered down with a case of Michelob and a sixty-four-inch football telecast, in an effort to forget that he had no homecoming reunion of his own. Not even one that took place in a frozen wasteland.

Mike burrowed deeper into the coat's raised collar. "I'm here, aren't I? Seven days of Christmas in a town called Christmas. Seven days of out-of-control holiday celebration."

Nicky gave him a look. An I-know-what's-frosting-your-butt look. "Buck up. There are no Scrooges in a Christmas Christmas."

"Yeah, yeah." Ordinarily, Mike was a doer, not a brooder, but he'd had a lousy year. First he'd been Dear Johned, then stranded for the holidays by a mother and stepfather who'd rather cruise Belize than gather around a faux fireplace in their Florida condo. Adding the recent news that his squadron would soon be sent on another tour of the Gulf had put him in an unusually morose mood.

He looked out at the barren landscape and said, with heavy sarcasm, "Another fine Navy Day."

"Hey, now." Nicky peered eagerly through the windshield, as if there was anything out there except more of the same. "Wait'll you see Shannon and the kids. They'll get you into the Christmas spirit."

"Don't worry," Mike said. One good, swift kick in the keister would jar him out of his malaise. "I'll be jolly for them. Ho, ho, ho."

While more than a year had passed since Mike had seen Nicky's family, they'd always be tight. There had been many good times, especially during the first years of duty after the men had earned their wings.

Mike was the godfather to the Yorks's first son, Charles, known as Skip. And Shannon had fixed Mike up with Denise, so they'd frequently double-dated with the Yorks.

At that thought, the fond memories might have turned sour, but Mike wouldn't let them. He focused on Nicky's kids instead. He was looking forward to being Uncle Mike again. Presents were wrapped and ready in his luggage.

There were also other family members to meet on this visit—parents, two sisters, assorted aunts and uncles. All of them ready to welcome Mike with open arms. Given his less-than-festive mood, the prospect was not entirely heartening.

Mike straightened. "What's that? That big, white thing?"

"What?" Nicky followed Mike's nod. "You mean the snowman?" He leaned over the steering wheel. "We're home."

The plywood snowman was fifteen feet tall, erected on the side of the road beside a placard that read Welcome to Christmas, Michigan. Mike stared as they drove by. The snowman's painted details were faded by time and a dusting of snow, but the message was clear. He was in for it.

"There's a Santa sign on the western end of town," Nicky said, almost apologetically.

Celebrate or bust. Mike geared himself up as they

drove toward a cluster of buildings that signified the outskirts of the town. Here was color at last. Every structure was strung with lights and decorated to the max. Bulbous, blow-up cartoon figures perched atop piles of snow. Plastic reindeer ran a roof line. Metallic man-made trees sat side by side with the real thing, all of them circled with blinking lights. The holiday banners that had been strung from the electric poles flapped in the wind.

"I ought to bring something," he said suddenly. "Like a…what do you call it—a hostess gift?"

"Don't bother. We Yorks are an informal bunch."

"No." Mike seized on a plan that would give Nicky and his family some private time. And himself, too. "When we reach the downtown area, drop me off. I'll nip into a gift store, then get a taxi—" He stopped abruptly, supposing that there were no taxis. "I'll hitch a ride, or whatever. If your family's place is close enough, I can walk."

"In this storm?" Nicky shook his head. The snowfall had thickened. Clumps of the white stuff had accumulated at the edges of the windshield wipers that swept the glass. "Mom would never forgive me. She's expecting you."

"Right—for dinner." Mike tucked a wool scarf into his coat collar and removed a pair of gloves from one pocket. "You want me to look bad, showing up empty-handed?"

"All right." Nicky braked. "I'll be back in an hour to pick you up." He pulled off the highway beside a mound of waist-deep snow. A couple of people bundled like penguins emerged from one of the lit-up buildings and waddled toward a stop sign that crowned another of the snowbanks. The street corner, presumably.

Mike glanced around. The smattering of buildings was still a smattering. "Where's the shopping district?"

"This is it."

"What about the downtown?"

"This is it."

"This is it?" *This* was nothing. The way Nicky had talked about his hometown's Christmas celebrations, Mike had expected a mini-Times Square, not a hodgepodge of humble businesses and homes half buried in snow. "You've got to be kidding me."

"Christmas is small." Nicky grinned. "But it's got a big heart." He pointed past the steering wheel. "There's the grocery, that's the post office and beside it is a gift store. The brick building across the street is a tavern called The Christmas Cheer. You can get warmed up there."

Michael stepped from the car and straightened. He took a gulp of the chilly air, smelling wood smoke as he looked from building to building. The tavern seemed to be the center of town—surrounded by vehicles, bursting jukebox music and activity. Three doors away, a white steepled church stood silent and closed, save for the tree sparkling with lights beside a signboard that listed service times beneath the spattered snowfall.

"See you in an hour, man." Mike shut the door, feeling road weary and run dry. Whether he was plunked in a Michigan snow pile or stranded on the arid mesas of Arizona where he'd grown up, small towns were all the same. Even when they came dressed in garish decoration.

"One hour, then," Nicky said with a nod. He gave a wave and put the car into gear.

Mike straightened his shoulders as he surveyed the town again. Travelers must have barely slowed down when they reached Christmas. A heavy foot on the gas, one blink of the eyes and they'd be out the other side.

A rush of wind sent snowflakes whirling. Mike tasted them on his lips. They clung to his lashes. He blinked and the swinging strings of lights that festooned the town turned to multicolored stars, blurry at the edges.

A second hard blink restored his vision. He was particularly glad of that when he saw the woman.

She was crossing the road, swept along by the wind. Her long, heavy coat flapped open. The tails of a red scarf whipped free, dancing like semaphore flags. Between the scarf and a matching knit hat pulled snugly past her ears was a fringe of golden-blond hair, molded to her pinkened cheeks.

The woman shot a clenched smile at Mike as she hurried past him and into one of the modest shops. She clutched a large leather purse and a paper gift bag with mitten-clad hands.

Pretty lady. A needle-sharp shot of interest made Mike's sluggish blood quicken.

He huddled in the cold, considering his shopping options. Severely limited. So why not follow her? The store she'd entered looked promising. Icicle lights danced from the eaves. A giant candy cane stood sentry at the door, twined in ribbon and evergreen garland.

A bell went off as Mike pushed inside. He stamped his feet on the welcome mat. The blond woman was at the cash register, chatting to the clerk while she shook snow off her hat and mittens. "My mother went and invited Oliver for Christmas dinner, since he'll be alone. I need to find him a last-minute gift."

The salesclerk, a rounded woman in her middle years, leaned over the counter and made a whispered comment. Both of them glanced at Mike, who was peeling off his gloves. "Merry Christmas, sir," said the clerk. Her smile was big and toothy. "I'll be with you in just a minute."

The blonde turned away before he got a good look at her face. "No rush," he said. "I'll look around."

The store was small. He prowled the rows of gift items, mainly Christmas-themed ornaments and such. He eyed the blonde over a rack of greeting cards. Something about her was arresting—her color, her brisk energy, the effervescent cheer that bubbled in her voice as she chatted about holiday preparations while fingering a display of fountain pens near the register.

"Finding anything?" the clerk called.

Mike nodded and pulled out a card at random. A cardinal in the snow.

He advanced along the aisle. Wrapping paper, twig reindeer, needlepoint Christmas stockings. Porcelain plates painted with winter scenes. Matching coffee mugs. What did a man without the proper Christmas spirit get to thank his best friend's parents for welcoming him into their home and holiday?

"Is it a fix-up?" the clerk asked her other customer. "You and Oliver?"

"Good grief, no." The blonde seemed alarmed by the idea. Her hands flashed over her hair before tucking a lock of it behind one pink-rimmed ear. A small gold hoop pierced the lobe. "In my situation? No."

Mike glanced away so he wouldn't be caught staring. *Situation?*

"Not even my mother, desperate as she is to marry me off, could think I'd possibly be interested in…" The woman shook her head in the emphatic negative.

Desperate?

The sales clerk clucked. "Then she's still on your case?"

"In her own way." A shrug. "You know my mom—she's so proper. This is hard for her."

"Well, she probably knows that Oliver's always had a crush on you. Just about everyone knows."

"Maybe he used to, but he must be over that. I was gone for years."

"Absence makes the heart grow fonder." The clerk's lips pursed. "Haven't you read any of his books?"

"The science fiction? Not in a long time."

"And the romances. He writes them under the name Olivia Devaine. You've been missing out."

The blonde's gaze skipped sideways toward Mike. He bent his head over the plate display. "Oh, dear," she said quietly. "I'm almost afraid to ask."

The clerk beamed. She was enjoying herself. "I've gotta tell ya. Every single one of his heroines bears a striking resemblance to you."

The woman groaned. "Are you certain you're not reading too much between the lines?"

"The latest one's titled *Marianne's Homecoming*. See for yourself." The clerk pulled a well-worn paperback from beneath the counter and tossed it onto the glass. "You can have it, if you want. I've finished. It's all about a lady executive named Marianne who returns to her hometown to stop an evil developer from bulldozing her family homestead. The hero is an investigative reporter."

With some hesitation, the blonde picked up the book. "That's not so very much like—"

"*His* name is Tolliver. Rand Tolliver."

"Please. Stop." She laughed. "Are there love scenes? I won't be able to look Oliver in the eye if there are steamy love scenes."

Colored lights winked off the lenses of the clerk's oversize glasses as she wagged her head. "There are a few kisses, but nothing explicit, darn it. Oliver's books never get too sexy. He closes the bedroom door, as they say." She hunkered down, her elbows on the counter. "If it wasn't for Dolly getting him liquored up at the Kiwanis picnic and taking him out to her van, he'd probably still be a virgin."

The blonde blinked. "That's old gossip. And private. You don't know what happened."

"I know that Dolly was hoping she'd get preggie so Oliver would marry her. She was certain he was rich, being a famous author, you know."

The blonde's head snapped back. Her cheeks had turned hot pink, but her expression was glacial. She yanked a fountain pen set from the display and set the case on the glass with a distinct click. "I'll take this. I'm sure a writer can always use a new pen."

"Oh. Um, hey, I'm sorry. You know I didn't mean anything by that."

"I'm sure you didn't." The blonde reached for her purse. "It's fine. Really. I'm not much in the mood for gossip these days, if you know what I mean."

Mike gripped one of the plates. He didn't know what she meant, but his curiosity was certainly roused. Suddenly he found himself hoping that the blonde wasn't secretly pining for that Oliver guy. Shouldn't matter to him when he was here for only seven days…except that seven days seemed a much shorter stay than it had fifteen minutes ago.

Christmas in Christmas might not be so bleak after all.

He walked toward the register with the plate and the card. The blonde's head dipped forward while she dropped coins into a zippered compartment of her wallet. She took her bagged item from the clerk and tucked that, the paperback book and the wallet inside her leather bag, not looking up until Mike stood right beside her.

"Thanks," she said to the clerk. Finally she glanced at Mike. He was six-one, but she was only an inch or two shorter in her stacked boot heels. A lovely smile flitted across her face as she nodded at him. Her nose was aquiline, with bold cheekbones set high in well-rounded cheeks. Her eyes were a dazzling blue that took his breath away. "Merry Christmas."

He made a raspy sound. "Merry Christmas."

She turned with a hitch of her purse strap and a

swirl of the nubby coat, yanking her red hat over her head as she departed. The bell chimed when she opened the door. A snow flurry swept inside, accompanying the blast of cold air.

Mike stared after her, even when she was gone. His pulse ticked like the ignition of a gas burner. Heat crawled up his throat. *There's something about her. Something very merry.*

"Didja find what you were looking for?"

"Uh, yes." He handed his selections to the clerk. "I'll take this and the card. Gift-wrapped, please."

"Sure thing. Let me get you a box."

Mike waited impatiently while the clerk boxed the plate and carefully wrapped the purchase in paper covered with candy canes. She chatted him up, managing to establish that he was only visiting and that the TV6 weatherman was forecasting a blizzard for Christmas Eve, three days hence.

"You mean this isn't a blizzard?" Mike asked absentmindedly while he fingered a couple of twenties. He'd pulled out his billfold to have payment ready even before the clerk had totaled the charges. He was being ridiculous. The blonde would be long gone by the time he reached the street.

But it was a small town. He could run in to her again.

The clerk chuckled while she rang him up. "You're not from around here, are you? This is a flurry."

"The only snow I've experienced was on a ski holiday in the mountains." His family had once been big on skiing vacations, but that had stopped when he was seventeen. He hadn't been back to the mountains since.

"Merry Christmas to you," the clerk called after him as he strode toward the door with his coat hanging open.

"And you," he returned.

The street was empty. Michael buttoned up, put on his gloves and checked his watch. Only five-thirty and the wan sun had completely disappeared. The streetlights had come on, illuminating the flakes that filtered out of the vast charcoal darkness above. He was stuck in a snow globe.

He tilted back his head. More of the snowflakes melted on his face and lips, but this time he didn't mind.

Let it snow.

A car pulled out of a small parking lot adjacent to the grocery store. Headlights cut across Mike's face, blinding him for an instant. Laughter rang out from the tavern as its door opened and closed. She might be there, toasting the holidays.

He was about to step over the snowdrift at the curb when he thought of the grocery store instead. *I should get wine. And chocolates for the sisters. There'll still be time to look for the blonde.*

The store was named Ed's Fine Foods and it was chockablock with overstocked shelves. The aisles were only wide enough for one cart at a time to pass among paths narrowed further by freestanding displays holding mismatched assortments of goods. Mike brushed the snow off his shoulders and stepped over a dirty puddle just inside the glass doors. He passed up the cart to take a handbasket and began to wend his way through the aisles in search of the liquor department.

A flash of red caught his attention. He made an abrupt turn, nearly smashing into a cardboard stand of chocolate syrup in squeeze bottles. By the time he reached the next aisle, she was wheeling her cart around the other end. He saw the nubby coat and the red scarf, both of them hanging loose, and dark blue jeans tucked into her stylish leather boots. She had long legs.

The wheels of her cart squeaked. He listened, sidling along the aisle until he was opposite her. The shelves were quite short. When he reached up and took down a box of bran flakes, he could peer over the top into the next aisle. She was reading the label of a bottle of champagne. With a sigh, she put it back and selected a different bottle for her cart before glancing over her shoulder.

Mike slid the bran flakes into their slot.

She looked up when he strolled into the aisle. He smiled. "We meet again."

"That happens often here. It's a small town." She pulled her coat closed, put both hands on her cart and nudged it over a couple of inches.

"I'm looking for a bottle of wine. What would you suggest?"

"There's not much choice. If you wanted beer—" She waved at the vast array. Towers of twenty-four-packs extended the section into the corner of the store.

"No, I need a good bottle of wine."

Her eyebrows made two precise golden-brown arches. "Trying to impress somebody?"

"An entire family."

"Then you should go top shelf."

He scanned the stickers and took down the highest priced bottle. Twenty bucks. Not *that* impressive. "I'll get champagne, too."

Reaching for the bottle she'd returned to the shelf, he grazed her arm. She inched away, looking at him out of the corners of her eyes. Her expression was thoughtful. "Big spender," she said with a gently teasing grin, before turning away and rolling her cart toward the opposite end of the aisle.

Mike's tongue felt unusually thick and slow. He still hadn't introduced himself, but he couldn't continue following her. Too obvious, even in a small store. He wandered the aisles, bypassing a sale on mixed nuts and waxed baking cups as he looked for the candy section.

A red mitten lay abandoned on the floor. The bottles in his basket clinked as he set it down to pick up the mitten. Smiling to himself, he turned it over in his hand. Soft and fuzzy, slightly damp.

He caught himself before he caressed the soft wool between his fingers. *Sap.* Embarrassed for himself, he thrust the mitten into his pocket. After the debacle with Denise, he wasn't planning to be in the market for a good, long while.

Except, technically, he was.

He loosened the scarf around his throat. The store felt too warm and close. Steamy. At least he'd found the sweets. He examined rows of chocolate bars and bagged candy that sold two for a dollar, looking for something, well, impressive. A small decorative gold tin of Whitman's Samplers was the best he could do, so he dropped several into his cart and headed for the checkout.

Wheels squeaked nearby. He sped up, making certain their paths intersected at the checkout lane. There was only one lane, and a woman with a cart filled with the makings for a holiday dinner—including a frozen turkey—had arrived first.

Mike lifted the turkey and a ten-pound sack of potatoes onto the conveyor belt, then turned and gestured at the blonde. Her cart stood between them. "Ladies first."

"No, you go. I have more items."

"I'm in no rush."

She nodded and moved past him. "Thank you."

"You're welcome." He stood directly behind her, looking at the straight, silky hair that brushed her collar. He closed his eyes and inhaled. How long had it been since he'd held a woman? Since he'd known the comfort of a soft, warm, curved body, a sweet voice and gentle presence?

He shook his head, dismayed that he could be seduced so easily, even after almost a year of virtual monkhood. First had come the long deployment, then the Dear John letter that had left him certain he'd never get serious with a woman again, let alone romanticize over a complete stranger.

One failed attempt was enough for him. At first marrying Denise had seemed like a good idea. She had all the qualities he hadn't known he was looking for in a wife, until she and Shannon had kindly pointed that out and convinced him to propose. Unfortunately, after they'd been together for more than a year with the wedding still on hold, his former fiancée had nagged and griped more often than not. The deployment to the Gulf had been the death knell to an engagement already on life support.

Many times since the breakup, he'd wondered why he'd done nothing, even though he'd recognized Denise's gradual withdrawal. And why, after the first sting of receiving her letter, he'd been more relieved than sad. More regretful than wounded.

Reminded of all that, he deliberately looked away from the woman standing in front of him. He told himself that his interest in her was only a pleasant distraction.

After a minute, he yanked the mitten from his pocket. "I almost forgot. You dropped this."

She turned halfway. "Yes, that's mine." She took the mitten, matching it with the mate. She smoothed them between long, elegant fingers with polished nails. "Thank you again."

"I'm Mike, by the way. Mike Kavanaugh."

Her mouth opened, then closed with a little *huh* of a smile. She glanced into his basket. "I thought you might be."

She recognized his name? Mike was going to ask how that could be, even in a small town, but she'd turned and begun placing her grocery items on the belt.

He studied her selections. Fancy stuff, fit for a more sophisticated holiday than he'd have expected, now that he'd seen the down-home, humble nature of the town. She had a loaf of Italian bread. Bunches of herbs. Fresh strawberries that must have been flown in. Jars of pistachios and almonds. Anchovies. Capers. Olives, radishes and two kinds of specialty cheese. Plus a bag of minimarshmallows and the bottle, which turned out to be sparkling ginger ale.

Marshmallows, anchovies and ginger ale? She had eclectic tastes.

She noticed his interest and paused with a jar of maraschino cherries in her hand. "My name is Mary."

He crinkled his eyes at her, despite the previous decision to keep his interest detached. "As in Mary and Joseph? That's appropriate for a town called Christmas."

"The villagers do take the name seriously," she said with a wry look.

"Maybe I'll catch the mood."

Her head cocked. "You're not imbued with the holiday spirit?"

The question made him recognize the loneliness of being out of step, particularly during the holidays. He was sorry for it, much more than when Nicky had pointed out the same. "Not lately, I'm afraid."

"Stick around. Christmas will work its magic on you."

"The town or the holiday?"

She smiled. "They go hand in hand."

She wrote a check for her groceries, then paused to put on her hat and mittens and button up her coat. She lifted one of her bags and reached for the other.

"Hold on," he said, liberating another couple of twenties from his wallet. "I'll help you carry those to your car."

She cradled one of the paper bags to her front

while he took the second and accompanied her to the door. The wind blew viciously, tearing the handle from her grip. The door banged against the wall. He pushed up close behind her and caught the door before it swung back into her face.

She sidestepped. "Do you need a ride? My car's around the corner."

"Thanks, but I'm being picked up."

They moved carefully along a sidewalk that was bumpy with packed ice and snow, then loaded the grocery bags into the backseat of her car, a red Mazda with a plump Santa suction-cupped to a side window. The license plate read FALALA.

Mary's eyes were slitted against the wind. She scraped hair out of her mouth and made a spitting sound. "I'll see you around then, Lieutenant Commander Kavanaugh."

He wanted to ask where and when, but stopped himself. "Maybe that can be arranged. I'm here for a week."

She hesitated, looking at him with puckered lips. Her eyes held a secret—something fanciful, as if she were playing with him. She seemed about to speak, but changed her mind and got in to the car instead, easing herself behind the wheel. She tugged at the coat, which kept her bundled as furry as a bear.

He briefly imagined what her body might be like beneath it. Long-limbed but curvy. For all the

willowy, athletic elegance, there was a solidness
about her, too. He sensed they would match up well.

Snow swirled. Wind whistled. He could delay no
longer. With reluctance, he said goodbye and
closed the door.

She smiled at him through the frosty glass and
started the engine. He stepped back, oddly forlorn as
the car pulled away, until he realized what she'd said.

Lieutenant Commander Kavanaugh.

After an instant of revelation, he gave a short shout
of a laugh. Some secret!

CHAPTER TWO

"Nicky!"

"Mer!"

Meredith York wrapped her younger brother in a bear hug and held on for dear life, having learned what the phrase truly meant over the past few years of their separation, particularly during his most recent deployment at sea. Her heart squeezed itself into a tight knot, then released as a wave of pure relief rolled through her. She let out a deep breath. At last.

She gripped his shoulders. "You're really here! You made it home for Christmas."

"A promise is a promise, Merrylegs." Nicky tilted his head back. He bumped their noses. "Don't cry."

"I'm not." She hadn't expected to be so sentimental, but Shannon and Mom were watching with red-rimmed eyes and watery smiles. In the background, Nicky's sons bounced off the couch with excitement.

"Where were you?" he asked.

"Mom sent me out for provisions."

Grace York dabbed the corners of her eyes with her apron, then retrieved the bags of groceries Meredith had dropped when she'd greeted Nicky. "My goodness. What's this? Goat cheese? Capers? What are we going to do with capers? I hope you didn't forget the marshmallows."

Shannon, Nicky's wife, had joined the siblings' embrace. She leaned her cheek against her husband's. "Skip and Georgie have their hearts set on church window cookies."

Meredith unwound herself. She rubbed her eyes. "Of course I remembered the marshmallows, Mom."

"Roquefort and goat cheese," Grace clucked as she rummaged through the groceries.

"I thought I'd make something different for tonight—hors d'oeuvres."

"Hors d'oeuvres. Fancy! Who are we trying to impress?"

Meredith flushed.

"She's got city taste now, Grammadear." Charlie York, the clan patriarch who'd remained fully involved in all activities since his retirement, stepped into the foyer with his sleepy granddaughter draped over his shoulder. At nine months old, Kathlyn Grace was the newest and much-adored addition to the family. "Don't fuss at the girl."

Meredith rolled her eyes as she slipped out of her coat and hung it on one of the wall hooks. She was thirty-six. Her hand went to her waist—her disappearing waist—as she bent to knock the snow off her boots. Certainly no longer a girl.

"Where's your friend?" she asked Nicky. Without considering why, she chose to keep her meeting with Michael Kavanaugh to herself for a while longer.

"At the Cheer. I'm going now to pick him up." Nick nuzzled his wife's ear. "Want to come along, honey?"

Shannon glowed. Seeing their happiness brought both thankfulness and a pang of longing to Meredith's heart. For more than a decade, she'd been satisfied with her thriving career as a human resources director for a large financial services firm, the high-rise condo she'd bought on Chicago's Gold Coast and her lengthy live-in relationship with Greg Conway, a financial analyst she'd met at work. Then, suddenly in the past year, everything had changed.

"Hurry back," Grace said. The slender, silver-haired homemaker was as active as her husband, involved in many church and community activities, in addition to her regular book club meetings and t'ai chi classes. "Dinner's in the oven."

"It's your favorite," Shannon said as she and Nicky put on their coats and boots. "Pot roast and mashed potatoes."

He moaned. "I can't wait. I've been dreaming about Mom's cooking."

Shannon paused while wrapping a scarf around her dark brown hair. "What about mine?"

He grinned wolfishly as she preceded him out the door. "You're in the *other* dreams."

Meredith gave Nicky another hug before he left, then stood in the farmhouse doorway, watching the couple drive down the long, dark driveway, until her mother complained that she was letting in the cold air.

I want that. Merry shut the door and absentmindedly straightened the jumble of the kids' snow boots, hats and insulated mittens. *There, Mom, I admitted it. I wish I was married.*

She'd lived with Greg for nearly seven years and had sworn up and down that a marriage certificate wasn't important to her. That had seemed honest, at the time. What she hadn't understood was how much the present situation would turn her previous perceptions topsy-turvy.

But would she marry Greg now, if he came back to her on bended knee? Definitely not. That ship had sailed. Only her mother still clung to the hope that there'd be a last-second wedding to save the day.

"Auntie Merry, Auntie Merry!" Skip and Georgie, her rambunctious nephews, burst into the foyer. "Grammadear said you'd help us make the church window cookies."

"Not tonight, I'm afraid. I have the hors d'oeuvres to do."

Georgie tilted his face upward. He was six years old, blond and freckled like his older brother. "What's 'oardurves'?"

She ruffled his hair. "Nibbly bits before dinner. Dolled up veggies and bread."

"Like crackers spread with Cheez Whiz," Skip said with authority. He was three years older than his brother and terribly sure of himself. With his father away on a sea tour, then on shore duty for the past six months, Skip had become serious about his role as man of the family. "And olives."

"Can I eat them?" Skip asked.

"You can try one," Merry agreed. The anchovy-and-pepper mix she'd planned for the *bruschetta* was sure to be too spicy for the boys. What had she been thinking? Her family was accustomed to plain home cooking, not the five-star cuisine she'd discovered in Chicago's best restaurants. They'd be baffled by *amuse bouche* and dumbstruck by dim sum. Her parents shared their insulated community's general distrust of visitors with sophisticated ways and a taste for change.

But I'm not a visitor. Meredith herded the boys to the kitchen. *I'm here to stay.*

When heart troubles had prompted her father's re-tirement at the same time her relationship with Greg was cracking like an overboiled egg, she'd returned to take over the family business. Thus far, every improvement she'd wanted to implement had been a struggle for control. Her parents had run the York Tree Farm since their wedding forty years ago, with Charlie overseeing the Christmas tree operation and Grace managing Evergreen, the seasonal gift and sandwich shop that served the cut-your-own-tree customers who began showing up in November.

Meredith glanced into the family room, where her father jiggled the baby on his knee while she goggled at the sparkling ornaments and blinking lights of the Christmas tree. In the kitchen, her mother hummed a carol to herself while seasoning a pot of frozen green beans.

They'll learn to adjust. Meredith smoothed the drape of her oversize cable-knit sweater. *So will I.*

After the elation of Nicky's return, her mood had turned into melancholy. Although surrounded by family, there were times that she felt very alone.

TWENTY MINUTES LATER, the pot roast was out of the oven and the hors d'oeuvres well underway. Meredith heard the stomping of boots in the foyer. She hastily pulled a pan of bread slices from beneath the broiler. "It's called *bruschetta,* Mom."

Grace flapped a pot holder at the wisp of smoke rising from a charred crust as if it were a spark from Mrs. O'Leary's lantern. "I know what *bruschetta* is, Miss Meredith. I watch the Food Network. All I'm saying is we don't need more carbs. I already have the potatoes and the rolls. Your father's diet…"

"I'll keep him away from the hors d'oeuvres." The cream and butter in the mashed potatoes was more of a concern, but Merry held her tongue. She took the pot holder and nudged her mother toward the doorway. "Sounds like Nicky's back. Go say hi to our guest."

Grace removed her apron. "You're coming, aren't you?"

Merry added chopped parsley to her anchovy mix. "As soon as I'm finished here."

Her mother paused significantly. "Nicky's pilot friend is single."

"I know, Mom." *He's also six feet of gorgeous, clean-cut masculinity.* "Don't embarrass him. The man's only on leave for a week. He's not looking to get involved with…" Merry gestured at herself. No other explanation was necessary.

Grace's face instantly clouded. She hurried from the kitchen without another word.

"Kryptonite," Merry muttered. She couldn't blame the woman for being old school, growing up as she had with strictly religious parents. And the wagons would certainly be circled if criticism came from outside the family. Even so, her mother's disapproval did make Merry feel self-conscious. She couldn't help but think of herself as Grace York's cross to bear.

"Merry," Nicky called from the family room, where the meeting and greeting was going on. "Come and see Mike. I want to show off my prettiest sister."

Meredith brushed off her hands and went to join the group. Her nerve endings were jingling and jangling like a triangle chorus, but she folded her arms across her midsection and put on a serene smile. She glanced at Nicky first, ignoring Michael Kavanaugh's presence. "You say that only because Noelle isn't home from college yet."

"Both my girls are lookers. They get it from their mother." Charlie put his arm around Merry's shoulders and urged her forward into the crowded room when she'd have rather hovered in the background. "Meredith, hon, this is Lieutenant Commander Michael Kavanaugh, ace pilot of the Blue Knight squadron. He flies a SuperHornet, an F/A 18E. They call it a Rhino."

"Yes, sir, but I'm not an ace."

"Not yet," Nicky put in.

There was no more delaying it. Merry pulled in a deep breath and looked up at the handsome Navy aviator. Her voice cracked, but she managed a placid, "Hello, Michael. How do you do?"

Then she put out her hand, waiting for the moment when the pleasure that had sprung to Mike's face at the sight of her would disintegrate into polite withdrawal as he got a second, closer look.

That didn't happen.

MIKE TOOK THE BLONDE'S hand and used it to pull her closer for a polite kiss on the cheek. "Fool me once," he whispered in her ear before retreating a few inches. He winked, then stepped away. She seemed defensive, not wanting to be crowded. "Nice to meet you, Meredith York."

Her smile wavered. "Call me Merry."

"As in Merry Christmas, or Mary and Joseph?" Amusement danced in his eyes. "How could I have forgotten that the Yorks are named by theme? Merry and Nicholas—though he's no saint—and what was the other sister's name again?"

"Noelle."

"Ah."

"Corny, I know, but blame my parents." She nodded her head at the beaming couple. "They're the town's unofficial Mr. and Mrs. Santa Claus, in charge of all things Christmas."

"Not even unofficial," Nicky said. His baby daughter was cradled in the nook of one arm. "I must have mentioned that my dad plays Santa at all the town functions."

Mike looked at Charlie. "Now I see why." Nicky's father was five-ten or so, and stockily built. Beneath a crop of gray hair, his face was flushed with good cheer and vigor. He could easily pull off an authentic "Ho, ho, ho."

Charlie winked as he tugged at his full gray beard,

which was liberally streaked with white. "I only grow it for the holidays."

"But Grampa's not the *real* Santa Claus," said Georgie. "He's an actor."

Mike caught the sly look that crossed Skip's face. He remembered informing his own younger brother of the truth about Santa Claus, after he'd put together hearsay with the hard evidence of the pile of presents they'd found stashed in their parents' closet. The five-year-old had been inconsolable for days, and Mike had been forced to give up a soccer game and endure a two-hour wait in line to visit Santa at the mall. After that, he'd kept the news about the Tooth Fairy to himself.

He squatted beside the boys. "Skip, it's been more than a year since I saw you, isn't that right?"

"Yes, sir."

"How old are you now?"

"Nine."

"That's pretty grown up. What about your brother?"

"He's only six."

"And you've been taking good care of him and Kathlyn while your dad's away?"

The boy nodded vigorously. "Uh-huh."

"Well done. I know your father's proud." Mike leaned a little closer. "I have a younger brother, too. He still remembers every holiday we spent together, but especially the visits from Santa Claus. You know what I mean?"

"I think so."

Mike clapped the boy's shoulder and stood. The other adults were talking about sleeping assignments and where the baby's pacifier had gone, but Merry had rested her hands on Georgie's shoulders and nestled him against her front. "You have a brother?" she asked softly.

"Steve. A civil engineer. He was in Mozambique, building a dam, the last I heard."

"And your parents?"

"My father passed away years ago. My mother is on a holiday cruise with her second husband." Mike quirked his lips into a smile. Casual, to show he wasn't as alone and lonely as it seemed…as he was. "Nicky took pity on me and hauled me along to join your family for the holidays."

"That's what I heard."

"Yeah?" He wondered what else she'd heard.

Merry's eyes opened wide. "Oh, shoot, I didn't mean that the way it sounded."

He laughed. "Never mind. Every Christmas party needs a poor little match boy."

Georgie had become restless. She gave the boy an extra hug and let him go, then clasped and unclasped her empty hands. "I'm—we're all very glad you could join us." She glanced somewhat warily at her mother. "One extra is no trouble, not when we usually have a half-dozen 'extras.' You'll see what a circus it is around here over the next several days. Our Christmas dinner is bedlam."

Her eyes were bright blue flames that he wanted to stare into until the image burned in his retinas. Instead, he glanced around the room, absorbing the comforting normalcy of the festive scene. A fire crackled in a potbellied woodstove. The furnishings were overstuffed and well-used. Colonial-patterned wallpaper clashed with the rug, while green and red holiday decorations added another layer to the visual chaos. The thick branches of the blinking tree reached to the ceiling. Already a large number of gifts had been placed beneath it.

"I haven't had a family Christmas in years," he said.

"You'll get one now," Merry replied, having followed his gaze. She was still fiddling with her fingers, holding them laced against her bulky green sweater. Her face was framed by a crisp white collar and the pale gleam of her hair.

The nervousness didn't suit her. She had a Madonna-like quality—gracious and gentle.

Except for the intense, burning eyes.

"I'm looking forward to it," he said, and meant it.

She smiled politely before turning her head aside. He couldn't figure out her bashfulness. She'd seemed self-conscious since they'd officially met, but she hadn't been like that at all earlier. What had changed? Being around her family? That was more the reaction of a high school girl.

"Who will show Michael up to his room?" Grace ignored the boys, who jumped to volunteer. "Merry, how about you?"

For an instant, she looked horrified. Then she dropped her lashes and politely refused the invitation. "Let Skip and Georgie do it. I'll get the hors d'oeuvres." She took the bottles Mike had brought and slipped from the room.

Mike found himself herded upstairs by Charlie and his grandsons. They gave him a small, simply furnished room under the eaves on the spacious farmhouse's third floor. There was a bathroom next door, and also another guest room that Charlie said Noelle would use when she arrived, since the boys had taken over her old room on the second floor.

Mike set down his sea bag, the large green Navy issued duffel. Although he'd shared many tight quarters aboard ship, close family living arrangements were something different.

The Yorks's house was filled to bursting. When Nicky had been shipped out, his wife and children had gone to live with his parents for the duration so Shannon wouldn't be alone with the boys during her pregnancy. Kathlyn had been born while Nicky was deployed, so this was only the second time he'd been able to spend a significant amount of time with her.

While Mike was no family man, he recognized that nothing was tougher than missing the first months of your child's life. A Dear John letter couldn't touch that loss.

"Where does Merry stay?" he asked the boys while unzipping his duffel. Charlie had excused himself to follow his nose to the kitchen and check on dinner.

"She has her own house," Skip said.

"It's by the tree farm." Anticipation glistened in Georgie's eyes when Mike pulled out three wrapped boxes.

He wanted to ask more about Merry, wanted to know everything, but he stopped himself. He had six more days.

"Why don't you two take these presents and put them beneath the tree?" The boys seized the gifts and Mike called, "Don't shake them *too* hard," as they galloped down the stairs.

He sat on the edge of the bed and raked his fingers through his hair. A day ago, he'd been stationed in San Diego, the aircraft carrier's home port, prepping for the next deployment. Sunshine and beaches contrasting with the heat of the tarmac and the blast of afterburn. Now this, a cold, white world pocketed with bursts of color and warmth.

His system was in shock.

He held his head in his hands, resisting the unexpected pull to take out Denise's goodbye letter. Hell, he'd read the thing a hundred times over the past months. Maybe more. He no longer missed his fiancée. He was way past that.

There was something else that tortured him, that wouldn't let him throw the letter away.

He took the frayed envelope from a pocket in his shaving kit and withdrew the letter. One measly sheet of paper. The end of a serious commitment should need more words.

Or not, when the engagement had already withered away to nothing.

Dear Michael...

Music from down below stopped him from continuing. He went to the door to listen. "Deck the Halls." Of course. The Yorks would play holiday tunes. They probably sang carols, too.

In fact, as he listened, a woman's voice joined the recorded music. Pure as a bell. He wondered if the singer was Merry.

The letter was crumpled in his hand. *Throw it away,* said his inner voice. *What good's it doing you?*

But he couldn't let go, not yet. He smoothed the crinkles and returned it to the envelope, then the envelope to its slot in his shaving kit. Moving faster, he undid a couple of buttons and yanked his shirt off over his head. Suddenly he wanted to be downstairs with Nicky's family, instead of alone and moping over promises broken long ago.

He took the kit and went into the tiny bathroom,

having to duck to use the facilities that were fitted beneath the slanted ceiling. He washed and quickly ran an electric shaver over his jaw. Deodorant. A touch of cologne. The pit of his stomach hollow, his senses on point.

Like getting ready for a date.

He left the shaving kit on the ledge of the sink and turned to go.

The staircase off the hallway creaked. He heard a footfall on the landing. "Um, Mike?" said a female voice.

After a moment's hesitation, he went back and grabbed the leather kit bag. *The damn letter.* He didn't want Merry to find it, even though one word from her, one meaningful smile, and he expected that he'd gladly forget it ever existed.

Outside, he almost bumped into Merry. She was bent at the waist, canted sideways, peering in through the partly open door to the guest room.

She jumped at his touch. "Oh! I'm sorry." Color rose in her cheeks. "I wasn't spying. That is, Mom sent me up to get you." Her gaze dropped to his bare chest, then shot upward like an elevator, right up to the ceiling. "But take your time." She turned away before he could respond, hastily removing herself from his half-naked presence, her boot heels clip-clopping on the wood steps. "We're having hors d'oeuvres."

"I'll be there in a minute."

He tossed the kit into his sea bag and pulled on a fresh shirt, smiling to himself as he tucked in the tails. He knew a little about Merry. She was older than Nicky by a year or two, and had been living in Chicago away from her family for years. An intelligent, successful woman, not lacking in experience. She wasn't likely to be thrown by the sight of a man's bare chest unless she had a particular interest in the man, and even then, he'd surprised her into the fumbling reaction.

Mike ducked to gaze into the mirror over the bureau, donned in gay apparel and suddenly bubbling with good cheer and a rousing interest that went quite a bit beyond the gentlemanly anticipation he should be feeling.

He touched his smooth jaw. *Fa la la la la.*

CHAPTER THREE

SHANNON PRESSED her shoulder into Merry's. "What do you think of Mike?"

"He seems like a nice man."

"That's all?"

Merry looked into her sister-in-law's eyes. She'd known Shannon all of her life, but they'd become much closer since both had returned to Christmas, sans the men in their lives. "Don't tell Mom?"

Shannon shook her head.

"He's…" Resist as she might, Merry's gaze was drawn across the table to Mike's face. He was handsome in a classic way, like an actor starring as a clean-cut war hero in a black-and-white movie, but it was his air of confidence that she found especially appealing. She'd always liked self-assured men. Even a little brash, as long as they could back up the attitude and didn't let it turn into arrogance.

"He's the entire package. Just about perfect." She dropped her gaze to her plate and stabbed a forkful of mashed potatoes. "I'm not sure that I can trust a perfect man."

"Greg wasn't perfect."

"This doesn't have anything to do with Greg," Merry insisted, but of course it did. Greg had seemed perfect to her for a very long time. She'd believed in him and their life together. Believed it much longer than she should have.

Shannon inclined her head, keeping to a low tone so they wouldn't be overheard. "They call Mike Captain America, you know. Cappy is his call sign." Nicky's was Boots, shortened from his original Father Christmas nickname.

"That's what I mean," Merry said. "He's too perfect. I am not."

"Yeah, but Mike went through his own breakup, remember? You've got that in common."

Shannon spoke as if that was a good thing to share, but how would she know? Nicky had been her high-school sweetheart. She'd never suffered a broken heart.

Merry shrugged. "Rebounding balls bounce *off* each other," she said thinly.

Her father's voice rang out from the head of the table, stalling the dinner chatter. "Merry, Shannon. Are you girls whispering about my Christmas present again?"

Merry's gaze snapped off Mike's face. She hadn't felt so awkward around her family since high school. No, even then she'd been relatively confident.

She had to go all the way back to junior high. Her first serious crush on a kid named Jason, who'd been a head shorter than her. Nicky had teased her without mercy. The family's enthusiasm had mortified her when Jason had arrived with his dad to escort her to an eighth-grade dance, with her mom snapping photos, her dad joking about first kisses and Nicky and Noelle making smooching noises behind Merry's back.

She smiled to herself. She hadn't thought of those days in years. The move back home had brought up a lot of old memories.

Shannon answered Charlie's question. "We're talking about sports."

"Sports?" Grace echoed with a genteel but dubious air.

Shannon smiled blamelessly. "Basketball."

"Our Merry was the MVP of her high-school class," Charlie said to Mike. "Basketball, volleyball and track. Her teams went to the regionals."

"Oh, Dad. That was ages ago. No one but you remembers."

Mike eyed Merry approvingly. "Do you still play?"

"I run, some. I golf during the summer."

"You look athletic."

Was he kidding? Everyone had stopped eating. She couldn't tell if there was an actual hush in the room, or if it was only her own ears that weren't functioning. Her voice did sound far away when she answered. "Not so much, lately."

Mike nodded as if he'd noticed nothing out of the ordinary. "There's really a lot of snow here. Do any of you ski?" Either he was oblivious, or extremely polite.

Merry let the conversation slide by. Her mother's face was pink. Shannon gave Merry a sympathetic squeeze before turning the other way to link hands with Nicky under the table. The men talked about the weight room they used aboard their aircraft carrier, while Charlie reminisced about learning Ping-Pong in 'Nam during his own tour of duty. Then he started in on his ski-jumping stories, which could end the dinner conversation if no one interrupted.

Merry told herself to relax.

"We built our own ski jump on Sawhorse Hill, a rickety contraption made of old barn boards and cedar poles. It leaned to the left. Climbing the ladder to the top was taking your life in your hands." Charlie eyed the last piece of beef on his plate, then reached for the gravy boat. "I volunteered to make the first jump."

"More guts than brains," Grace said fondly, as she always did at this point in the story.

"A trait of the York males," Shannon added, making Nicky give a raspy chuckle.

Perhaps a trait of the females also. Merry frequently felt as if she was teetering on the brink of a scary adventure, with no one to catch her when she fell.

She looked at Mike. He was watching her father, nodding along with the story. Skip and Georgie sat on either side of him, lured there by Mike's intervention when the boys had started fighting over who got to sit next to their dad. He'd called them his dinner service copilots.

Diplomatic, decent, dependable. Not to mention dishy. Merry felt slightly feverish whenever she thought about catching Mike shirtless, and since she thought of *that* every five minutes, well, no wonder she'd grown so warm.

She tugged at her collar while her gaze rose inexorably from the surface of the table. Yes, he was still there. Captain America, a practically perfect man. Her unexpected gift for the holidays.

Who'd arrived in her life at the worst possible time.

"So there I was at the top of the makeshift ski jump, on a couple of badly warped skis," Charlie continued. "The ramp was as bumpy as a backwoods road beneath the snow we'd packed onto it. Someone gave a push to get me started."

Charlie surveyed the table, in his element. The only thing he liked more than telling family stories to a new audience was gravy. His gaze fastened on Mike. "Do you know ski jumping?"

"Sure. Like the Olympics?"

"Well." Charlie chuckled. "We young pups thought so at the time. After dinner, Grammadear will take out the photo albums. There are a few shots of me in the glory days."

Shannon nudged Merry. She mouthed "Help." Dragging out the albums and the same old stories would lead to an entire evening of family time.

Merry nodded. She remembered well. Some fathers kept their daughters' boyfriends in line with threats. Her dad did it with endless storytelling until the boyfriend *du jour* went away out of sheer boredom.

"What happened then, Grandpa?" Skip made a swooping gesture. "Did you fly through the air with the greatest of ease?"

Charlie put his fists beneath his chin. His shoulders hunched. Georgie and Skip hunched with him. "I started down the hill. Picking up speed. The spectators were shouting. 'Jump, Charlie, jump!'"

Merry looked tenderly at Georgie, who was entranced, his eyes like glass marbles. Mike was doing the same. Their gazes intersected. They exchanged smiles and the heat flushed through her again, only this time she wasn't thinking about Mike's physique, but what a natural inclination to fatherhood he seemed to have. He was the type of man—strong, quietly confident, even heroic—that any woman would like to have as the father of her children.

Hormones. Merry clutched the napkin in her lap. Even considering that Christmas was the season for miracles, she was getting carried away.

"Snow was flying," Charlie continued. "The boards rattled beneath my skis. One of them popped up beneath me as I hit the end of the ramp."

Georgie gasped.

"I shoved off with all of my might, snapped my arms out and cranked the skis up to my chin as I leaned into the jump." Charlie extended his arms and did an airplane maneuver over the crowded table. "I must have flown for a mile." He winked at the grownups. "The spectators cheered. And then—" he focused on the boys "—I dropped out of the sky."

"Bam," said Skip, slapping a fist into his palm.

"I hit hard, you betcha. Nearly bit my tongue in half. One of my skis snapped like a twig and I went head over heels." He drew circles through the air. "Cartwheels, I did. All the way across the landing zone."

"Were you hurt, Grandpa?"

"Nope. A snowdrift saved me when I landed in it headfirst." Charlie's chest expanded. "I set the hill record on that very first jump and nobody ever did beat it."

Skip's eyes narrowed with skepticism. "How far did you fly?"

"Eh. The exact number's in dispute because we didn't have a tape measure. About…" Charlie inched his hands apart like a fisherman with a tall tale. "Forty feet. Give or take."

"Wow," Georgie breathed.

"More giving than taking, is what I've been told, my dear." Grace rose. "Are we having second helpings? Thirds? No? Then, who wants to help me clear?"

Both Mike and Merry started to get up, but Shannon shot to her feet, dragging Nicky with her. "We'll do it. You sit down, Grammadear." She handed her husband the meat platter and potato bowl and swept up several dinner plates, escaping through the swinging door between the dining room and kitchen.

A short silence settled among those left at the table.

Skip's expression was solemn. "Mom and Dad want to kiss in the kitchen."

Merry pressed her lips together, but she caught Georgie's eyes. They giggled.

"Silly," Grace said with a bemused smile.

"I already caught Mom and Dad kissing on the staircase," Skip informed them. "They didn't even have the mistletoe."

Mike straightened. "There's mistletoe?"

"You rascal." Charlie chuffed. "Look out, ladies! I know how these jet jocks operate." He waved a finger at Mike. "Don't even think about stealing a kiss from my pretty gal. You hear me, Grammadear? I'm giving orders. You're to stay away from this one."

Grace's eyes shined behind her bifocals. "Oh, Charlie."

"Uncle Mike can kiss Aunt Merry," Georgie said.

"No, he can't," Skip corrected. "Because—"

"No one's kissing me," Merry interrupted. She laughed awkwardly. "I've sworn off mistletoe for the duration."

Mike studied her from across the table. "Got a boyfriend?"

She gathered silverware. "No."

"She's gonna be a single—"

"Skip. That's quite enough, young man," Grace interrupted smoothly despite the high color in her cheeks. "You and Georgie take the rest of the plates into the kitchen, please."

"Knock first," Charlie joked.

Merry couldn't bring herself to stand, not when Mike was looking at her so closely. Curiosity was written across his face. She'd begun to believe that he hadn't noticed what seemed so obvious to her—obvious and slightly embarrassing. She was her mother's daughter.

"Woodstove needs stocking," Charlie said with a harrumph. "Let's go into the family room. We'll get out those picture albums I mentioned."

"Sounds good," Merry said, making a motion to rise. *Any* distraction sounded good.

While Mike went to pull out her mother's chair, Merry dropped her napkin and bustled about clearing the table before following the others toward the archway that opened to the family room.

Mike glanced back at her over the tops of her parents' heads, silently signaling for a wingman.

She nodded, sympathetic to his plight. Although she'd rather head home, she couldn't desert him, despite the likelihood that her brief fantasy of a Christmas romance was about to sputter and die like a neglected fire.

"I'll be along in a minute," she said. *In all my glory.*

She sighed. The warmth had been nice while it lasted.

MIKE STOOD WITH Meredith in the enclosed entryway of the farmhouse. The walls were paneled in knotty pine, with what seemed like a hundred family pictures hung in random configurations above the rows of coat hooks. While he held Merry's coat out for her, his gaze skipped through the annual class pictures, following her from white-blond pixie haircuts and toothless grins to poufy marshmallow hair with lots of lip gloss. Apparently, she'd had no awkward teenage phase— only clear skin and a shining smile.

"Let me walk you home," he said.

She pulled her hair free of the collar. "You don't have to. It's only a quarter mile down the driveway, then a short turn off the highway."

"But it's snowing. And dark."

"I can manage."

From the family room came the sounds of Charlie scraping ashes in the stove. A cabinet door closed and the lights went off in the kitchen. It was not even 9:00 p.m., but the Yorks were closing up the house for the night.

On their way upstairs, Nicky and Shannon stopped to glance into the entryway. "Good," he said. "You're walking her home."

"Her?" Merry jammed the red knit hat down to the tips of her ears, which peeked through the strands of her hair. "She's walking herself."

"Meredith, don't be stubborn."

She looked at Nicky. Her lips twitched with a sassy retort left unsaid. From their many long talks aboard ship, Mike knew that the siblings had always been combative with each other, but it seemed that Merry wouldn't argue tonight.

"All right," she conceded. "You win. He can walk me home."

"Take care of her like a brother," Nicky said to Mike with a wink.

Merry made an inarticulate sound of frustration. "Argh." She was shaking her head and smiling at the same time, a gesture similar to one Mike would direct at his own brother.

"You look like an elf," he said when Nicky and Shannon had disappeared up the stairs. He couldn't resist touching a finger to the pink curve of Merry's exposed ear. "An aggravated elf."

She rearranged her hair, brushing away his hand. "Are you saying I have big ears?"

"No, pointy ones."

She fingered a lobe. "Really?"

"Maybe a little." For a couple of seconds, he watched her fiddle, sliding the hoop earring through tender, pierced flesh. His breathing became shallow. The small gesture was unexpectedly intimate. Almost erotic.

He wanted to lick her lobe with his tongue. Brush away her hair and kiss the downy skin of her nape.

They'd sat on the couch for the past hour and a half, with Charlie between them. Whenever he'd gotten up to poke at the woodstove or sneak another Christmas cookie, one of the boys or even Grace had taken the empty place before Mike could slide closer. Sitting quietly among the chatter about family history and town happenings, Mike had been content with watching Merry. She'd contributed a few wry comments and hearty laughs; she had a wonderfully full, rich laugh that rang like a bell. But for the most part, she'd been subdued, not the bold older sister of Nicky's stories.

Mike remained intrigued. Why was she holding back?

"I have to walk you home," he said. "I need to stretch my legs."

What he really needed was to walk through the falling snow, holding hands with a woman who didn't quite make him forget his self-imposed isolation and the impending deployment, but who somehow seemed to give a more meaningful sense to it all. Perhaps he felt that way because his arrival in Christmas had revived his patriotic protectiveness for hometown America. Or maybe not.

What he knew for certain was that for now, for one quiet moment, he wanted to think only of Meredith and how good it would feel to be the man reflected in her bright eyes.

Her lashes lowered, then lifted, almost in slow motion. He thought he could hear the soft brush of them against her skin. Her lips parted. "Mike. I'm sorry about that—spending the evening on the couch with my parents, not able to get a word in edgewise. We're all a bit overexcited about having Nicky home."

"I enjoyed it."

Her musical voice dropped an octave. "You don't have to be polite with me."

"No?" He moved closer.

Her eyes widened. "What I meant is…" She stopped and laughed with a slow chuckle that danced along the surface of his skin. He felt her nearness in every follicle and fingernail and heartbeat. "You know what I meant."

He took the red scarf off a hook and looped it around her neck, then let his fingers drift across the first buttons of her coat as if he meant to do them up for her.

She crossed her arms. Looked away. Defensive and evasive once more.

Grace popped her head into the entryway. "Good, you're still here. Hold on just a sec." She bustled away. "I'll give you leftovers to take home, honey."

"No!"

Grace returned, looking askance.

"I don't need leftovers, Mom. Keep them for the men." Merry gave Mike a nod. "Hot beef sandwiches for lunch."

"Mmm. That sounds great."

"At least tell me you'll join us?" Grace inquired of her daughter.

"I'll be working." Merry explained for Mike's benefit. "I'm running the family business, the tree farm and the little shop where we serve hot drinks, sandwiches and cookies. We get a spurt of sales from the last-minute customers, these final few days before Christmas."

"If you're sure you'll be busy, I can send one of our Navy heroes down with a sandwich." Grace twinkled her eyes at Mike. "You'd do that for Merry, wouldn't you?"

"Of course."

She gave his shoulder a pat and said her good-nights, closing the inner door behind her.

Merry shrugged. "It's a sandwich shop. I don't need a homemade sandwich. But there's no use arguing."

He cheerfully agreed. "No use at all."

The door opened again. Charlie, this time, blustering. "Didn't intend to interrupt you two, but I just wanted to say good night. And to give my man, here, a word of advice." He pumped Mike's hand, leaning in to whisper in a not-very-hushed voice, "Look up."

"Oh, for—" Merry broke off her exclamation and whirled away, reaching for the outer door as Charlie exited through the other.

Mike looked up. On a long loop of ribbon, a clump of mistletoe dangled beside the old-fashioned light fixture.

He reacted instantly. But while he had the honed reflexes of a fighter pilot, Merry had gained a good head start. She flung open the door.

The cold air slammed into Mike like a wall. His lungs instantly seized but he got the words out. "Don't you want me to…kiss you?"

She hesitated at the threshold, shooting him a quick glance. "Not like this." And then she was gone.

He followed her across the frosty planks of the front porch. The railings were hung with thick evergreen swags. Strings of bulbous red and green lights traced the columns and eaves, making the sky beyond the drifting snowflakes seem very black.

"Hold on a minute." With his bare hands, he grabbed a shovel that had been left by the door and moved past Merry to clear the fresh snow from the front steps.

She stood at the top with her hands on hips, back

swayed and stomach protruded. "*Tsk*. Where are your gloves?"

"In my pocket. In my coat." He finished scraping. Snow clotted the corners. "In the house."

"Go and put them on."

"Promise you'll wait?"

She gestured with her mittens. "What am I going to do—outrun you?"

He cocked his head. Curious. "You might try."

She looked away, withdrawing again as she wrapped her unbuttoned coat around herself. "Go. You're shivering."

He took the steps two at a time, snatched his gear from the coat hooks and was back beside her before the vapor of her breath had dissipated. "You didn't answer my question," he said as he shrugged into his coat. "Don't you want me to kiss you?"

"I answered."

"Was that an answer? 'Not like this?'" He didn't put on his gloves. His fingertips were tingling, all right, but not solely from the cold. "Not like what?"

A frown puckered her lips. "Not with my parents pushing us together so obviously. Not with you leaving in only a week. Not when we're both…pressured by the circumstances."

He loomed over her, nudging a finger beneath her chin, making her look at him. He dropped the timbre of his voice to a conspiratorial level that was only partly joking. "What are these circumstances you speak of?"

She blinked. "You don't know?"

"I feel like I've walked in to the second act of a play without a script."

He could see her roll the words on her tongue, but she didn't say them. Instead, she stood taller, lifting her chin away from his touch. "Nicky never told you about me?"

"He told me lots of things. Like how he used to call you Merrylegs, after the fat pony in *Black Beauty*. That he once hit you in the elbow with a rubber-band airplane and gave you a small scar. How proud he was that even though you were a successful executive in Chicago, you gave it all up to move home after your father's health problems. And that you and the guy you lived with split up around the same time." Mike had grown more serious, the last fact putting gravel into his voice. "Is that what you mean? Are you still brokenhearted?"

The cold air was no match for the block of ice that was suddenly lodged inside him. Was she aware that they were both on the rebound and therefore ripe for a foolish fling that would certainly be a mistake?

"I'm not brokenhearted," she whispered.

"Me, neither."

She licked her lips. "But I am…"

"Eminently kissable," he said, and gathered her

into his arms so she couldn't run away again. "Even without the mistletoe."

He put his cheek near hers. Taking his time. Feeling the warmth as their breath intermingled, which he could actually *see* happening. There were stars in her eyes, brighter than the ones that sequined the sky. Amazing.

The wait was excruciating, and delicious. That was not a word he'd used for anything but food before now, but it was right. Meredith was alluring, enchanting and delicious—even before he'd tasted her.

Finally she conceded. Her eyes flickered and she moved a fraction toward him with her lips.

He took her mouth with certainty, pressing a firm kiss against her chilled lips. For one heartbeat, she hesitated. Then her mouth softened and warmed for him, became a sweet, welcoming haven.

Pleasure grew inside him like a cadence—slow and sure. He wasn't keyed up the way he felt at the controls of his jet, soaring with adrenaline. Instead, kissing Merry was knowing himself in ways he'd neglected lately. It was feeling the solid earth beneath his soles while angels sang in his ears.

He deepened the kiss. Her body swayed into his. He dropped his hands to her waist, wanting to feel every inch of her against him. He reached into the warmth beneath her open coat, stroked his palms down her sides, framing the roundness of her belly as he looped his arms around her.

Ding. A bell went off in his head.

Plink. The penny dropped.

Click. Pieces came together.

He stepped back, needing to see what he'd somehow, incredibly, managed to miss up until now.

"Meredith."

She looked straight at him, nodding a little.

"You're pregnant."

Her hands went to the bulge beneath her sweater. It was a small one, not so difficult for a distracted man to miss. Still, he felt like a half-blind Mr. Magoo, groping for soda-bottle glasses.

"Yes," she said in such a smooth yet sharp-edged voice that his vision snapped back into crystal clarity. "I am pregnant. Expecting, as they say." Her mouth flattened. "In a delicate condition."

She might have warned him. Her, or Nicky, or—

Oh, hell. Mike stopped the excuses. He had only himself to blame for falling for her in the span of a single evening.

She had pulled her coat closed again and was standing rigid beneath the neon glow of the Christmas lights, her head held at an awkward angle as she studied him for a reaction.

"Well, I'll be damned." He summoned up a reckless grin to deflect his sense of shock and, yes, disappointment. "Fool me twice."

CHAPTER FOUR

MERRY THRUST HER HANDS into her pockets and strode along the driveway, kicking up clumps of downy snow. Cold air lodged in her lungs, and she huffed, hurrying faster and faster. Puffs of vapor floated from her mouth.

She heard Mike behind her. "Wait for me."

"I'm fine." She raised her fists and pumped her arms. Any other time, she'd have given him more of a run for his money. Well, perhaps not *any* other time. A few months from now, she'd be waddling.

He caught up and took her arm. "It's really dark out here."

"That's how it is in the country." There were no lampposts or streetlights, even at the main road. The lights from the farmhouse had been reduced to winks and blinks among the trees.

Mike slowed, his head tilted back. "But, man, take a look at those stars."

She resisted his friendliness. "I've seen them."

He kept hold of her. "Indulge me. I'm a city boy."

"Don't give me that." She stopped anyway, trying not to breathe too hard. "You've seen stars before, and closer than most of us get." She thought of him at the controls of a strike fighter, zooming toward a midnight heaven, and felt a thrum on her heartstrings.

"Sure, but they look different here."

"How so?" She tipped her head back, taking a deep breath as she gazed at the black sky dotted by a zillion diamond-chip stars. The Milky Way was especially sharp and vivid.

Merry's defensiveness abated. Mike's easy way, even when she'd been snippy, was a comfort.

"Clarity," he said. "I've never seen stars look quite so bright and sharp. Must be the cold air."

She shuddered.

He put his arms around her, no longer looking at the sky. "Let's get you home." His voice was low and intimate, giving her another small shiver, but one that came from the inside.

They walked, following the curved driveway through the trees to the point where it reached the main road and split off toward her small cottage. He kept one arm around her, holding her snugly against his side as they matched their gaits. The residue of her ire dried up.

"I'm sorry," he said.

"Forget it."

"I was surprised, that's all. I don't know how I didn't notice sooner."

"I wondered. But I'm not at the 'Wow, you're huge!' stage."

He hesitated. "How far along?"

"Five months plus." It'd happened the past summer, if Mike was counting. She'd moved home for good in the early spring and had gone back to Chicago just once more, to finalize the sale of the condo. After the closing, Greg had asked her out for drinks. She'd known that wasn't a good idea, but Greg was persuasive, coaxing her with talk of how if only she'd change her mind about moving they might get back together. They'd wound up spending the night together in her hotel room. "For old time's sake," he'd called it the next morning, no longer pretending there was anything but residual fondness remaining between them.

By August, she'd known she was pregnant, and by the autumn she'd made a bargain that left her completely on her own.

Her and the baby, alone together. Which was what she'd thought she wanted.

As they walked in silence, she watched Mike from the corners of her eyes, wishing again that they could have met under different circumstances. Their feet crunched on the packed snow of the shoulder of the main road, which had been freshly plowed.

She touched her tongue to cold lips. "So Nicky didn't mention my pregnancy?"

"Nope."

"I suppose sisters aren't hot topics aboard aircraft carriers."

"You'd be surprised." The admiration in his tone was pleasing to her—and surprising.

"Maybe he didn't know how to explain it." She'd put her family on the spot, with her pride and independence.

"Explanations aren't necessary." Mike smiled. "I know how it happens."

She glanced over. Silver moonlight outlined his sharply handsome profile. "You're not curious about the circumstances?"

"I didn't say that."

He was right—she didn't owe explanations, at least not to him. Then how come she felt as if she had to say something? Make a declaration that would set down her parameters?

So he'd know whether or not to cross them.

She tucked her chin into her collar. "I'm pregnant and I'm not marrying the father. He's out of my life—completely. That's all you need to know."

"He doesn't want to share in the life of his own child?" Mike said in a disbelieving tone that bordered on scorn.

"He says no."

"Huh." Even a grunt could pack a lot of meaning. It seemed that she and Mike shared the opinion that Greg was a shortsighted fool.

"But you're protec—um, keeping him a secret? Was it someone local, like that Oliver guy you were buying a present for?"

"God, no. Oliver is just a friend. He's been around for a long time. Before I moved back home, I hadn't seen him in years." She glanced at Mike again, remembering him prowling the aisles of the gift shop while the clerk had blathered on about Oliver's books. She hadn't figured out who Mike was until the grocery store. "But you knew that, didn't you?"

"I'm putting two and two together."

"More like one and one," she said, her voice rough in her throat. "There's just me and the baby." She hadn't planned that, and as the pregnancy progressed, she'd grown to realize that she didn't particularly want it that way, but she was too sensible not to accept the situation for what it was. No girlish dreams or romantic wishes for her.

"Just you and the baby," Mike repeated. He glanced at her. "What about family friends who kiss you on the porch? Don't they count even a little?"

"Them?" She tried for a carefree chuckle. "There have been so many. I lose count."

He was silent as they turned before reaching the road that continued on to the business area of the tree farm. Instead, they took the narrow lane that led to her place, which was tucked among a grove of snow-laden evergreens. The commercial trees stretched in rows across several big pastures, lined up like sailors with their white "dixie cup" hats and epaulets of snow.

They arrived at her little house, a periwinkle-colored cottage with white trim and plum shutters. It was old and small but charming, built in the 1920s with just one bedroom and a tiny telephone nook off the dining room, which she intended to remake as a nursery. "This is me."

"Cute. But it's not you."

"Oh?"

"I'll bet you had a modern place in the city."

She thought longingly of her condo's polished wood floors, on-call maintenance men, the granite-and-stainless-steel kitchen with ice maker and garbage disposal, the slate fireplace that ran on gas—no muss, no fuss, switch it on, switch it off. Her life in Christmas was like a wood-burning stove—more work, rather messy and unpredictable, but heartwarming and good for the soul.

"Look at that." Mike gestured at the rough-and-ready Jeep parked in her driveway. The vehicle was practical for running chores around the farm and town, but too drafty for winter driving.

She raised her eyebrows at him. "Not me, either?"

"What happened to the Mazda with the license plate?"

"Falala? That's my mother's car. My father's plate reads Hohoho." The walkway narrowed between knee-high mounds of shoveled snow. She stomped her boots on the front steps. "It seems that you think you know me pretty well."

His gaze strayed to her middle before he brushed a few flakes of snow off her shoulders. The corners of his eyes creased when he smiled. "I'm only making a few educated guesses."

Her hand went to the fullness of her belly, hardly noticeable in her thick Berber coat. She was still getting used to the idea of the pregnancy displaying itself without her consent. Before she'd started showing, she hadn't had to deal with the curious stares around town, or the endless speculation. In another month or two, she wouldn't be an individual at all. She'd be a walking baby announcement.

No man would look at her then.

Especially not the way Mike had, with masculine interest, his eyes deepening as he speculated about her as a physical, sexual being. She'd enjoyed the flirtation, the attraction, and was pleasantly surprised to see that hadn't entirely disappeared even though he'd cooled a few degrees.

Of course, the mutual interest wasn't going anywhere. Even the notion was ridiculous, although wasn't it just her luck to meet Mr. Right when she was so very clearly in a state of Miss Taken?

Or just plain *mistake*.

Except, with every day and every flutter of the

baby growing inside her, she considered the child less and less of a mistake.

Her baby was a gift. Granted, a gift at a surprise party. One to which it was too late to invite a guest as disruptive to her plans as Lieutenant Commander Michael Kavanaugh.

She put her hand on the doorknob. "Thanks for walking me home."

"My pleasure."

"I hope you enjoy your stay in Christmas."

His head bobbed. "I had my doubts at first, but now I believe that I will."

She looked steadily at him, returning his intense stare, keeping the longing out of her face with a tremendous effort. The kiss had been nice—extremely nice—but he couldn't still be interested!

"Don't forget that I'm pregnant," she warned.

Surprise flickered over his features. "What are you saying?"

"That I'm not…" Interested? She couldn't pull off that large a fib. "I'm not available."

"Then the father *is* in the picture, even if it's only emotionally."

"No. He's not. Don't be obtuse. I'm telling you that you're better off catching someone else—someone who's not preggo—under the mistletoe."

"That's too bad." He squeezed her upper arms, looking for one instant as if he were going to lean in for another kiss before he moved away, backing down the steps.

She was left all alone, clutching herself, and wishing that things could have been different.

He paused, cutting a stirring shape, there in the moonlight with the stars caught in his eyes and every heart-wrenching word from his mouth rising white in the air. Ghosts of what might have been. "Can we be friends, at least?"

"Of course." She smiled, even though her upbeat mood had dipped at hearing the "just friends" line from him so quickly. Despite discouraging herself, she'd hoped for more.

"See you tomorrow." He waved. "Go on, get inside before that baby of yours asks for a thermal blanket."

She opened the door and turned as if to go in, but she didn't. She stayed and watched Mike's retreat until the dark, quiet forest had enveloped him.

"I HEAR HE'S FIFTY kinds of handsome." Jackie Marshak drew a tall cup of steaming liquid from the hot chocolate machine, then sprayed it with a mini-mountain of whipped cream while simultaneously reaching for a red paper napkin.

Her talent at multitasking was why she'd worked full-time at Evergreen for the past seventeen Christmases. The seasonal job was a fill-in to her irregular income as a self-employed machine repairwoman.

The Yorks had seen Jackie through high school, trade school, two marriages—a child from each—and an equal number of divorces.

"Who?" A customer Merry didn't quite recognize accepted the mug that Jackie had placed on the counter. She was an older lady, probably someone Merry should know, except that it seemed during her years away all women in her mother's age bracket had merged into one. Typically, they had short gray hair, lined faces, big glasses, puffy winter coats, pleasant smiles—and way too much curiosity.

"Merry's brother's friend," answered Jackie. "He's a Navy pilot, too. Visiting the Yorks for Christmas."

"Ooh." The woman's avid eyes peered at Merry through the steam on her glasses.

Jackie nodded. "Single. And a dreamboat."

"I'm not in the market," Merry said to Jackie between clenched teeth, keeping her voice below the uneven hum of the hot chocolate machine. The appliance was ancient. Only Jackie's talent with widgets and doohickeys kept it running.

"Maybe you're not, but I sure am." Jackie gave the side of the hot chocolate dispenser a hearty slap.

Merry held her breath until the *chugga-chuggas* evened out. She was hoping to eke one more season out of the motor. Although she'd installed a new microwave and a line of gourmet hot chocolate made with scoops of chocolate candy bits that melted into hot milk, the traditional drink remained their bestseller. The residents of Christmas were traditional types.

Maybe if her store manager pushed the new flavors as often as she gossiped....

Merry made busywork for herself, refilling one of the chrome-capped straw dispensers. "Who told you about Mike?"

Jackie wiped up brown droplets. The hot chocolate machine leaked; the white laminate counter beneath its nozzle was permanently stained. "My cousin was in the Cheer last night. Your boys bought a round for the house, making them very popular."

"You're telling me that Chex Marshak noticed that Mike is 'fifty kinds of handsome'?"

"Chex is secure in his masculinity." Jackie pushed back the fluff of her curly black bangs and grinned with her palm plastered to her forehead. "Maybe he didn't use those exact words." She nudged Merry with an upraised elbow. "So is he?"

Merry gave a sideways nod. "Only forty-nine kinds."

"Shoot." Jackie swung a fist through the air. "Why do men always fall short of my expectations?"

They laughed. At thirty-three, Jackie was younger than Merry and not particularly cultured or adventurous. She'd never moved away from Christmas, even commuting for the trade-school course in machine repair after her first divorce. Yet she'd seen and done things that Merry had yet to experience. They'd bonded over Jackie's homegrown solution for morning sickness and imaginary acts of revenge against ex-husbands and bad boyfriends, turning a respectful working relationship into a damn fine friendship.

After a glance out the windows to check on a couple of stragglers who were picking and choosing among the remaining cut trees, Merry retreated to her office. She'd taken over a cubbyhole off the back of the one large L-shaped room that housed the café counter, half a dozen tables and the gift shop area.

She sat at the computer and tapped a key to remove her tropical beach scenes screen saver. The spreadsheet of the past several months' shipments came up. Her parents had kept their makeshift books at home, using an adding machine to total the season's receipts over doughnuts and coffee. She'd carted all of the paperwork to the office and planned to work her way through the shipping records, entering them into her database so that eventually she could open the appropriate spreadsheet and see at a glance how many blue spruce they'd shipped to Indiana five years ago.

She studied the troubling figures of the year's shipments. The ongoing trend toward fake trees worried her. When she'd asked her father about the drop in sales, he'd brushed off the concern by breaking off a twig of balsam and waving it under her nose. "Smell that," he'd said. "People don't want plastic when they can have the real thing."

Jackie popped in. "Someone's looking for you."

Merry swung around. "Mike?" The name shot out before she could censor it.

"Oliver."

"Oh." Yikes.

Jackie smiled bravely. Merry suspected that her friend harbored a secret crush on Oliver Randall. Hinting about it had turned Jackie unusually taciturn. She'd muttered something about him being too nerdy for her. What she meant was *smart*.

"I don't suppose…" No, Merry couldn't say she was busy. Oliver was a good guy, not at all pushy. He was too shy and humble, in fact. Nevertheless, his unrequited crush made her uncomfortable. She needed to find a way to get him to look at Jackie instead.

She tapped keys. "Why don't you give him a cider or chocolate on the house? I'll be right out, soon as I finish up here."

"Sure thing." Jackie put a hand in the front pocket of her peppermint-striped apron, took a deep breath and turned on her heel. She'd upbraid a supplier who was one straw short on a delivery, yet meek, quiet Oliver Randall tied her tongue like a cherry stem.

Merry returned to the computer, allowing one minute to stretch into ten. When she finally emerged, Jackie had vanished. Oliver sat slump-shouldered at the counter, staring into an empty mug with a rim of foam.

"Hi, Oliver. Want a refill? Where'd Jackie get to?"

He looked up, his glum expression brightening considerably. "She went out. Told me to hold down the fort while she was gone, but there aren't any customers so I've just been sitting here, plotting."

"Plotting?" Not how to ask her out, Merry hoped.

"A new book. I'm working on something different—a mystery."

The reclusive author was as close to a celebrity as Christmas got, though he wrote in multiple genres under so many pseudonyms that only the most dedicated fan could keep track.

"Who done it?" Merry asked lightly.

Oliver pushed up his glasses, thick ones that gave him the wobbly eyed look of a stuffed animal. "That's what I'm working out. Poison's been done to death."

Merry wondered if he'd ever considered contacts or laser surgery. Oliver was not entirely unattractive, if you looked past his lack of confidence, the receding hairline and longish locks that were often disheveled in a "mad genius" way. On the plus side, she'd never heard him raise his voice in anger. He fed stray cats. His mind was inquisitive, and he'd almost solely funded the town's library-on-wheels program.

"How about electrocution? Jackie could help you out with the research."

"Electrocution, hmm?" Oliver's expression became distant as his work in progress recaptured his attention. When he wasn't holed up, writing, he was often spotted on long, rambling walks about town, lost in thought.

Merry had her doubts about a matchmaking attempt. Oliver's fictional world seemed more vital to him than reality. Jackie Marshak was definitely a live-in-the-moment type of woman. Then again, maybe each of them was exactly what the other needed.

"Go see Jackie's workroom at her house. She has all these decapitated vacuums and gutted toasters strewn about. You could be inspired to come up with a really unusual murder scenario."

"I might do that." Oliver's gaze briefly fastened on Merry before sliding away. He nodded toward the windows. "I, uh, came for a Christmas tree. What type should I get?"

"You can't go wrong with the traditional blue spruce or white balsam."

"Is that what you have at home?"

"Um." Merry had been too busy with the business to unpack her Christmas decorations. She'd been telling herself that the cottage was too small for a tree, that putting one up wasn't worth the bother when she'd be spending most of the holidays at the farmhouse. Heaven knew *those* halls were decked out to the nines. "We have a spruce."

"Then that's what I'll get."

"What about ornaments? Do you have enough of those?" Merry waved at the gift section. "We've got a wide variety, many of them made locally. Why don't you pick out a good selection, really do your tree up right?"

Oliver's mouth puckered. "Okay, sure."

"I mean, if you need them."

"I guess I might." He ambled over to the colorful shelves, looking rather lost. "There are some boxes in the attic," he mumbled to himself, "but I don't know if…"

Activity in the tree lot distracted Merry from making the sale. Mike was there, holding up a tree while a family circled, examining it from every angle. Jackie was at his elbow, gazing up at him while she chatted. She was only five-two and petite, cute as a button even in her big old khaki parka.

The unwanted twinge of jealousy came as a shock. Merry ducked into the office and snatched up her coat and hat. "I'll send Jackie back in to help you," she called to Oliver as she sailed through the door.

AFTER THE FAMILY had driven off with an eight-foot balsam roped to the roof of their car, Mike leaned in toward Merry and said, "There's a roast beef sandwich in my pocket."

Her eyes widened. "And here I thought you were just happy to see me."

He smiled. "It's from your mother."

"Subtle, isn't she?" Merry put the money in the cash box at the plywood sales stand. Jeff Martti, the young man who handled onsite sales, returned from helping a couple who'd cut their own tree. She introduced him to Mike, then gestured at the four-wheel ATVs parked nearby. They used them to ferry customers through the groves on searches for the perfect Christmas tree. "Would you like the tour?"

"Sure, if you're my guide."

She nodded a little too eagerly. Seeing him with Jackie had given her a jolt. Acceptance of her situation was practical; passivity went too far.

Merry turned. "Everything under control, Jeff?"

"Yeah." Tall and gangly, Jeff was a college student and also her sister Noelle's longtime boyfriend. "We're not too busy, but it'll pick up by late afternoon when people are getting home from work."

"Why don't you go in and get warm while you have a chance? We'll have the ATVs back before long."

She started to give Mike the basic instructions for driving the vehicle, but he stopped her. "I thought we were riding together."

Together? Holding on, hugging?

She buttoned up her collar. "There's no need."

He gestured with his head. "Come on. I'll drive carefully."

"*You'll* drive?"

"You don't trust me? I fly million-dollar jets for a living."

"It's not that. It's…" *Holding. Hugging.*

She shrugged and handed him the ignition key. "Whatever you say. We can ride around the tree lot here, then head up to the far groves so you can see the harvesting operation."

"Great." He hopped onto the ATV, as enthused as Skip and Georgie when they got to drive the vehicles, though he waited for Merry to settle in behind him before he started the engine.

"Take it slow," she shouted above the noise. "The rows are plowed, but—"

The rest of her words were lost as the ATV shot forward with a jerk. The motion threw her back, then forward against Mike. She gripped his waist.

"Sorry!" He slowed to putt-putt level as they moved in between the first row of evergreens. Here and there were the empty spaces where trees had been freshly cut, the snow trampled flat around the sorry-looking stumps that remained.

She'd always felt sad, looking at them. All the years of growth and careful pruning—ended with a few swings of an ax or the bite of a chain saw. Worse was seeing the trees discarded at curbs all around town after their brief time of glory, most of them trailing with a few wan pieces of tinsel or mangled popcorn garland.

In Chicago, Greg had wanted an artificial tree, and she'd almost given in to him for all the practical reasons that made so much sense, stopped only by the family vow that had been drilled in to her since birth. *Yorks don't do fake trees.*

Speeding up with a rousing shout, Mike drove them in and out of the rows, following the paths like a maze. The grove ended, opening to a pasture that rose on a gradual incline to a ridge that overlooked the front acreage of the farm.

They stopped there, the engine idling while they looked back over the way they'd come. "From here, you can't tell how many trees have been cut," Mike said. "It looks like a normal forest."

The sky was a rare wintry blue, nearly cloudless. Sunshine glistened off the crust of the snow-thickened slope. "We replant in the spring," she said. "Filling in the gaps."

"I know trees are a renewable resource, but does it ever make you sorry, seeing them cut down?" He made a face. "That was dumb, right? I probably sound like a naive city boy to you."

"No, actually, you don't." She tightened her mittened hand on the fabric of his coat. It had remained bunched in her grip; she hadn't let go when they paused. Maybe because holding on to his solid, warm body felt so good. She hadn't been this close to a man in months. "I've always felt that way, too."

"Yeah. Makes me think of the line from the Judy Collins song—something melancholy about Christmas coming and they're cutting down trees." He glanced at her over his shoulder. "But you're okay with it, right? Enough to run the business, anyway."

She shrugged. "Family obligation." He didn't respond, so she went on, compelled to explain. He was easy to talk to. "It's not so bad. I'm looking forward to updating the operation, if my Dad will let me. I've implemented a few changes already. We need to diversify if we're going to thrive."

"There must be a long downtime, between seasons."

"Dad always kept busy. There's planting, and pruning. Grove management takes more work than you'd think. By late summer, we're settling our contracts for the season. We cut and ship trees, starting in the early fall, plus garlands and wreaths. The local sales are small potatoes, but fun for the community."

"You're planning to stay for good, then?"

"I—I think so."

"Hmm." Mike turned to eye her, obviously noticing how she'd faltered. "It's not really you, is it?"

She shook her head, which wasn't an answer. "You forget that I grew up in Christmas. Being away for so long, I'd sort of forgotten how great a small town can be. Everyone's friendly and laid-back. No pretensions. No pressure. And it's safe here. There aren't many better places to raise a child." She realized that she was persuading herself more than him.

"I can't argue that."

"Shannon's hoping that Nicky will want to move back, when he leaves the Navy. Maybe not to Christmas, but somewhere close enough to visit often." Merry nudged Mike. "What about you? What are your plans for the future?"

He gunned the engine. "I haven't thought about that yet. I may stick with the Navy."

"Ah, a career man. Or are you one of those devil-may-care types?" She felt a little confrontational, perhaps because the divide between them seemed so immense. "I hear that most of you jet jocks get addicted to the danger, speed and adrenaline. You develop a live-for-the-moment outlook."

"The danger is something you have to accept. I'm not addicted. Maybe a little, lately, but for me it's always been about flying. The flying is what drew me to the job." He straightened, glanced back at her. "Hey. It's cold. We'd better get moving."

Although there'd been much left unsaid, she was ready for a change of subject. She waved a hand. "Follow this ridge. There's a road through the trees down there that'll take us to the big groves. You're in luck, because we're up and running today, getting ready to truck a small order downstate overnight to a retailer with an unexpected shortage. That almost never happens this close to Christmas, but I'm doing them a favor because they were running an advertised promotion."

Mike nodded and they took off again. "Pick it up," she called. "Snow's deeper here. We have to plow through fast or we'll get bogged down."

Boys with toys, she thought, though her own exhilaration heightened as he gave a *whoop* and gunned the gas, propelling them through the several inches of powdery snow that had accumulated overnight. The fat wheels of the ATV threw up a cold, white mist that showered them. Merry dropped her face against Mike's back and held on tight, even as they descended into the forest, where it was dark and peaceful beneath the drooping branches.

She smiled to herself.

Hugging.

Holding.

Hoping.

CHAPTER FIVE

AT THE TREE FARM, they dismounted. Two part-time workers were running a truckload of trees through a large orange baling machine. Mike became enthused, as those with XY chromosome were prone to be, over the activity and noise.

They showed him how each fresh tree was loaded onto a conveyor belt that fed into a funnel on the machine. The tree emerged on the other end with its branches flattened beneath a tight envelope of plastic webbing. They would spring back up again after being unwrapped.

Mike pitched in. Merry tried to lend a hand, as the trees weren't that heavy, but he insisted that she should take a seat on the ATV. Before he could bring up her "delicate" condition, she retreated, smiling over his enthusiasm for the physical labor as the men finished up the order. Even after the fun part was over, Mike heaved the packaged trees onto the truck and helped secure them for the drive to lower Michigan.

After a brief discussion, the workers climbed into

the truck and departed. The round trip was over six hundred miles. They planned to drive all night and return the next day, unless they hit bad weather. Merry had agreed to pay double time to make up for the last-minute run. The workers were grateful to have the extra income in time for Christmas.

"Your gloves are ruined," Merry said when Mike walked over to her, grinning widely. He brushed pine needles and snow off his shoulder epaulets. "And look at your coat! That's pitch. It's impossible to get out."

"Pitch?"

"Tree sap."

"No problem. I'll bring the coat to the dry cleaner's."

"We don't have a dry cleaner in Christmas. My mother uses rubbing alcohol on my dad's work clothes, but there's a reason they're called work clothes." She plucked at the sticky stains on the front of his previously pristine military topcoat. "I'm sorry. I should have warned you."

"Don't worry about it. I had a good time."

"Hauling trees?" She'd have teased him if she wasn't so impressed by his vigor. There was something about a man being all physical that made her more aware of being a female. As if she needed the reminder, these days. "I didn't expect you to do so much, but thanks. You got the guys off to an early start."

"I enjoyed it—being out in the fresh air, working

a few muscles." He surveyed the baling machine with satisfaction. The hot motor steamed in the cold air. "I didn't realize you had so many employees."

"There's even more to the operation than you've seen. We have harvesters and drivers. Throughout the fall we also buy boughs by the tonnage from local cutters, then hire other part-timers who turn the greenery into the garlands and wreaths that we sell. Almost everyone is a seasonal employee."

"So they don't get benefits?"

"I'm afraid not. We have worker's comp, and I give several of the long-term employees an extra stipend to help them pay for health insurance. That's as far as my budget stretches."

"I wasn't scolding you. Just trying to get a grasp on how things run."

She nodded. "It's a different world, up here. No pensions, no perks. Many of the townspeople work several jobs. Whatever it takes to keep them going. Christmastime is the town's best season for tourists, naturally, but the snowmobilers visit as long as there's snow. Then come the summer outdoor enthusiasts."

She didn't know why she was talking so much, except that the way Mike looked at her so closely was unnerving. She wanted to impress him with her savvy and strength. "Between the weather and the low incomes, life in the U.P. is not for weaklings." Did that sound like a complaint? "I admit that I miss my old salary and the conveniences of the city, but there are other compensations."

"Like?"

"Community. The slow pace. Fresh air and sunshine."

"It is beautiful here, I'll give you that. I'd like to come back in the summer."

She tilted her head to return his bold look, but became unexpectedly self-conscious and had to glance away. She studied the tree tops, watching as a sunwarmed clump of snow dropped from a high branch, landing as softly as a pillow. "Maybe someday you will."

His gaze lowered. "You'd have had the baby by then."

She hesitated, not accustomed to discussing the pregnancy so freely. To avoid questions, she'd fallen into the habit of keeping most of her joys and worries to herself. Only Jackie and Shannon were her confidantes.

"I'm due around the end of April."

"A spring baby."

"Mmm-hmm."

"You shouldn't be alone." After the words were out, Mike got a funny look on his face. The color in his already ruddy cheeks darkened. "That isn't what I meant…exactly."

She didn't want to know, especially because she

suspected he hadn't meant to volunteer. Her throat stifled as if stuffed with cotton batting. "Well." She coughed. "No need to concern yourself. I'm not alone. Don't mistake my mother's reluctance for complete disapproval. She's looking forward to the baby. She only needs time to adjust to the circumstances."

"That's not what I was talking about." Mike stopped himself, apparently rethinking putting his two cents in. "None of my business," he added gruffly.

They returned to the tree lot. "Time for a hot drink," Merry suggested with a lilt as Mike put out a gentlemanly hand to help her off the ATV.

His gaze lingered on her face. "You've got color in your cheeks."

"So do you."

"Healthy living."

She pressed her mittens over her cheeks. "Or impending frost bite."

Inside Evergreen, Jackie greeted them from behind the counter. "What can I get you?"

Merry looked at Mike. "Hot cider? Gourmet hot chocolate? We have coffee, too. And there are muffins, cookies, sandwiches, soup."

"Surprise me."

She hung their outerwear on a rack by the door, pulled out the gloves he'd stuffed in his pocket and spread them out to dry. The foil-wrapped sandwich came with them.

Jackie kept an eye on Mike while she prepared a plate of cookies and the cider Merry had asked for. "Sure looks like you two are getting cozy."

"He wants to be friends," Merry whispered.

"Crap. How do you feel about that?"

"It's the best idea, don't you think?"

"Yeah, sure. Don't think I didn't notice how fast you moved your butt when you thought I might get my hook in him." Jackie made a casting motion, then handed the invisible fishing pole to Merry. "Here. You've got a bite."

Merry wouldn't play along. She dumped a scoop of gourmet chocolate chips into a mug and put it into the microwave. "Sorry. I turned in my license about five months ago."

"IT'S YOURS," Mike said, pushing the sandwich plate toward Merry. "You need the nourishment."

She widened her eyes at him. "Why? 'Cause I'm preg-n-ant?"

"Shouldn't I say that?"

"Seems funny," she said with her mouth full of roast beef and homemade bread. "We barely know each other."

"You sure of that, Merrylegs?"

She ripped off another bite. "Nicky has a big mouth."

"We have a lot of downtime aboard ship. He's told me stories."

"Then it's your turn."

"What do you want to know?" He spread his hands. "Ask away. I'm an open book." Why had he said that? There were areas of his life he wasn't ready to examine, especially with her. He must be out of his head, carrying on with the flirting while claiming it was only friendliness.

He had less than a week's stay in Christmas. She needed someone who could commit to the long haul.

Merry chewed, holding a napkin near her mouth. He glanced around the café, taking in the homespun decor. The place was all red, white, green and Christmasy, from the painted wood tables to strings of lights hung from whitewashed beams.

"I suppose you have been mentioned over the years," she said. "I must not have been paying enough attention. All I seem to know is that you and Nicky met at flight training in Texas, were assigned to the same squadron and that recently you were—" She stopped abruptly and became overly interested in the remaining half of the sandwich, opening it to rearrange the slices of beef smeared with yellow mustard.

"I was dumped while we were on our last cruise," he said. "Dear Johned, to be specific. It happened months ago and I'm over it, but Nicky felt bad that I was going to be alone for the holidays. That's why I was invited to Christmas for Christmas."

"You don't seem too heartbroken."

His brows quirked. "Fighter pilots don't cry."

"Be serious. Shannon said you were engaged to a great girl."

"Yes, she was. We had a lengthy engagement—a year and a half."

"Wow. That's a long time." Merry considered that for longer than it warranted, her mouth pulled into a knot. Finally she shook her head and picked up the sandwich, making a visible effort to relax. Her shoulders sank at least an inch.

He wondered.

"What was her name? What was she like?" Merry nibbled at the sandwich. "I hope you don't mind me asking."

He picked up a warm cookie. Chocolate chip with dots of red. "I don't mind." He bit. Dried cranberries. "Her name was Denise. I met her in San Diego, through Shannon. She was—is—a good woman. She managed a home furnishings store for a big chain. We shared a few interests, like music and sports. She even got to enjoy going off-roading with me." He shrugged.

"And I'll bet she was pretty." Merry's tone was even, without a hint of envy. He wouldn't have minded a *hint*.

"Denise was plenty attractive, but not like you."

Merry blinked.

"I mean, she was more typical. Brown hair and eyes, tanned, fit, a trendy dresser. You're…" He met Merry's vivid gaze and knew he couldn't say out loud that she made him feel as if he'd been punched in the gut by a heavyweight boxer. "Never mind."

She stole a glance at the woman at the counter. Jackie, he remembered. A plainspoken live wire who'd looked him over like a cow at the county fair. She was listening to every word they said.

Merry tapped the table. "You haven't tried the hot chocolate."

"Right." He stirred the melting whip cream into the drink, then laid the spoon aside and took a swallow. The chocolate was unusually rich and thick and spicy.

"Wow," he said. "That's got bite."

"You said to surprise you." Merry grinned. "It's one of our new flavors—Aztec chili pepper. *Muy caliente.*"

He tried another sip. "Not bad. But next time, surprise me a little less."

"You don't like it."

"No, it's tasty. But I'm more of a—a—" He read the chalkboard menu above the counter. "A Black Forest man."

"I'll get you one." Merry lifted a hand to signal for Jackie.

He stopped her with a touch on the wrist. Just a touch, and even that gave his senses a jolt and his lungs a squeeze. "Next time."

"Next time," she agreed with her eyes on him. Too

bright, too blue, too incisive. He had the feeling she'd read between every one of his lines.

"You and Nicky spent a lot of time in the Southwest," she said. "I thought you'd have a taste for spice."

"Sure—burritos and chimichangas. I didn't expect to sweat over a mug of hot chocolate."

She smiled, saluting him with her cider. "It is pretty tangy."

He chugged half the mug, then put on a show of mopping his forehead with a sleeve, making her chuckle. His tongue burned.

They each ate a cookie. "About your former fiancée," she said slowly. "Can I ask why you broke up?"

"Why *she* did—is that what you want to know?"

Merry nodded. "I'm having a hard time understanding," she said, as if it was a concession.

Perhaps it was.

"Let's see." He raked a hand through his hair. "The thing was, our relationship came too easy. It was comfortable. We used to double-date with Nicky and Shannon. In fact, they both urged me to pop the question, which seemed a good idea at the time."

Merry made a sound in her throat. "But you must have loved her, to ask her to marry you."

"I did." He nodded, although the relationship seemed to have occurred a long time ago. An early chapter in a book that was just getting to the good part.

He continued. "There wasn't enough passion to sustain us, especially after I was deployed to the Gulf. Denise and I tried to keep up, but you know how it is, maintaining a long-distance relationship that wasn't that strong to begin with."

Merry straightened. "How *could* she, when you were at *war*—"

He cut her off. "No, don't blame Denise. The timing wasn't the best, but that couldn't be helped. We both knew the engagement was dead. She happened to be the one who pulled the trigger."

Merry went directly to what was, for him, the heart of the matter. "Why didn't *you* pull it, if, as you say, the engagement was already over?"

"That would have been dishonorable."

Her expression was conflicted. "Would you have come home and married her out of politeness, if she hadn't said anything?"

"No." He was definite on that point. "But I would have eased into the matter, face-to-face."

"That's no better." Merry's hair flew as she gave a vigorous head shake. She tucked it behind her ears. "Ripping off the bandage fast hurts, but not as bad as the slow torture method. Trust me. I know."

"That's right. You've gone through a recent breakup, too."

"Not all that recent. When my dad had the heart attack last winter, Greg and I were already on the outs.

Moving back home was exactly the clean break I needed to make."

"Almost a year ago," Mike mused. He'd counted Merry's old boyfriend as the most likely father candidate, but the timing was out of whack. Unless they'd given their romance a second try.

"Yes," she said, adding with deliberation, "ten months and two weeks, give or take a day or two."

"And you two were together…how long?" He could make a few points of his own.

She narrowed her eyes as if he'd just swished a shot taken from the top of the key. "Six, seven years. Around there."

"A long time." Without getting married. Her making a sour face over his prolonged engagement made a little more sense. Pacified, he tossed an easy shot at the basket they'd been circling. "Were you planning to marry?"

"Marriage wasn't an issue, for either of us." Her tone was firm but clipped, cutting his initial speculation short.

So she wasn't feeling jilted. Then what about the "slow torture"? And where did the baby fit in to the picture? Could it be that she was as mature and well-adjusted as she appeared?

The bell over the door chimed and a group of tree buyers entered, bringing good cheer and the cold air. Merry took advantage of Jackie's distraction with the bustle to lean forward and speak directly to Mike alone.

"Just so you know." She did not quaver or blink. "Greg Conway will never be the father of this baby."

Slam dunk.

HOURS LATER, at home, Merry's emotions were still churning. She'd enjoyed the afternoon jaunt with Mike very much, but what had started out as a friendly chat had become serious the instant he'd mentioned his long engagement. In her mind, Mike had been immediately linked to Greg, even if that wasn't fair.

Objectively, she recognized the situations were different. Mike was in the military. He was called away for months at a time. And at least he'd been willing to make the commitment, then unwilling to break it lightly.

He was not Greg.

I'm lucky we never married. She thumbed through her closet, looking for a suitable garment to wear to dinner at her parents' house. *We were so alike on the surface, but marriage would have been a disaster.*

Maybe she'd always known that. When they'd first parted ways, she'd bitterly blamed Greg for failing to make the commitment that might have helped them ride out the rough patch. Later, she'd admitted that she'd gone along with living together, persuaded by his reasoning and too proud to suggest that she might, just maybe, want the legal bond. In actuality, living together had deflected her own reluctance to take that final step.

Being pregnant and single made a woman take a stark look at her life, both past and future. Merry had seen that she wasn't opposed to all marriages, only to her and Greg's. Down deep, she'd known he wasn't the one.

Her clothes from her old career weren't right. Neither were the silk blouses and skinny little tanks and camisoles she used to wear for dressy occasions.

She stripped off her sweater and shivered in the cool air. With the price of heating oil at another all-time high and her nest egg socked away in mutual funds and government bonds to guarantee her baby's security, she'd taken to keeping the thermostat low.

"Mike's not Greg," she said to her reflection in the closet mirror as she held up a designer dress she'd worn to evening work events. Cocktail parties at executive homes, fancy fund-raisers where the exorbitant tab was picked up by the company. Much too dressy for the U.P.

"Time to buy new clothes." She tossed the garment aside. Looked at herself in elastic-waist crepe pants and a bra from an expensive lingerie store. It seemed to be shrinking. "Maternity clothes."

Good grief. Maternity clothes.

Maybe she could get through the pregnancy in elastic waistbands and men's flannel shirts. For now, jeans would do, even if she had to leave them unzipped and fastened with a safety pin. She dug through her drawers for her fat jeans, a thicker pair of socks and a bra that held in her newly abundant breasts.

So what if Mike wasn't Greg? She'd still sensed his reluctance. Toward Denise, toward her. He'd held back nearly as much as he'd flirted, frozen in the "just friends" zone by the news of her pregnancy.

Not that I can blame him. Merry cupped her baby bump. Recently, she'd begun feeling the baby's movements. Butterfly flutterings that brought up strange and overwhelming emotions. She'd felt her heart expanding, swelling with a greater capacity for love, a deeper commitment to cherish and protect.

And there'd been no one to tell, not the way a woman could speak to her husband or lover.

"Shut up." She yanked on a turtleneck and a shirt that still buttoned, made from a butter-soft suede chamois in the palest shade of fawn. "You don't have a husband and you don't need one, either."

Not Greg. Not Oliver. Not Mike.

Not anyone.

She was capable on her own. How ironic when she'd finally discovered that she had more to give than she'd realized.

THE DINNER BEGAN LIKE a repeat of the previous evening, as the family milled around by the front door, greeting a new arrival. Nicky's sister, this time, who was home from college for the holidays.

Mike stayed out of the way, until Skip latched on to his hand. The simple gesture made him feel like one of the family.

"Hi, Mike." Noelle's smile was huge. She looked a lot like Merry—a tall, pretty blonde in a blue ski jacket with the lift ticket still attached. She squealed and jumped onto her toes to give him a hug. "I remember you!"

He hugged, then set her back. "That's right. You came to San Diego once for a visit."

She'd been only seventeen then, a stunning girl who'd attracted lots of attention at the beach and the officer's club. Certain doggish pilots in their squadron had begged Nicky to bring her back when she turned twenty-one. Maybe eighteen, some had said, which had sent Nicky into big-brother mode. He'd vowed to keep Noelle away from them for good.

"You've grown up," Mike said with a smiling glance at her brother.

Noelle slipped out of her jacket. Had she ever grown up. "I'm twenty."

"Still not legal," Nicky pointed out.

Noelle smirked and swung a waist-length ponytail across her back. "Close enough."

Skip piped up. "Is No-No getting arrested?"

"Only for arriving late," Grace said with a *tsk*ing

sound. She herded them toward the family room. "And having too much fun on her way home."

"Sorry, Mom, but the skiing was great." Noelle looked back at Mike while she was led away by the boys. "Do you snow board? Marquette Mountain's not too far away. We can squeeze in a day trip."

"I've skied, but never tried snow boarding." He'd wager that she was a fast slider.

She clapped. "Then you need to learn! I would love to teach you."

The door opened and Merry arrived, stomping her boots on the welcome rug. Mike's senses gave a leap of recognition. He only had time to take her coat and mumble a hello before Noelle was launching herself at her sister with open arms. They were a huggy family.

After a few minutes, Mike excused himself and went upstairs to the guest room to give the Yorks some private family time. While they were too warm and welcoming to ever consider him an interloper, occasionally he felt like one anyway.

Taking out the Dear John letter would only make him melancholy. He resisted the urge and went and stood at the window. Blue shadows striated the snowy fields. His thoughts drifted toward his own family.

When was the last time they'd hugged? Too long. He hadn't seen his mother in a year, his brother longer than that. They got along fine in a once-a-month phone call kind of way, but they weren't particularly close. And hadn't been in almost seventeen years, which, by no coincidence, dated to his father's death.

Oh, hell. Talk about melancholy….

Mike closed his eyes. The family had been on an autumn vacation, staying in a remote mountain hut with plans to hike, fish and canoe. The cabin had no running water, but there'd been propane to provide heat and power the appliances. Four days, they'd planned to stay, daring rapids, steep trails, grizzly bears.

So many ways to have an accident. Dying in bed on the very first night, supposedly safe and sound, hadn't even seemed an option.

A shudder wrenched Mike's eyes open. He stared bleakly, then touched a finger to the corner of the windowpane, where frost had grown in an artful pattern that looked like mold spores. His body heat melted a round spot through the thin layer of ice.

He'd awakened, although to this day he didn't know why. He remembered struggling out of a drugging sleep, not quite realizing what was wrong, but knowing in his gut that it was something bad. He'd shaken Steve awake, hauled him out of bed, screamed in his face to get him moving.

In the adjoining bedroom, his parents had looked like corpses—pale and blue in the moonlight. He'd broken a window, trying to get it open. Carried his mother out. Sucking the cold mountain air into his lungs had cleared his head.

He and his brother had gone back for their father. Too late.

Sounds came from the bathroom next door, flushing, the gurgle of the faucet. Mike pulled his hand off the window. The tips of his middle fingers were numb; they'd melted three spots on the window pane.

Merry paused outside the bedroom door, the way he'd known she would, considering that she could have used either of the downstairs bathrooms but had climbed up to the third floor instead. She leaned against the jamb, her arms crossed over her middle. "Watcha doing?"

His fingers tingled. "Nothing."

She nodded. "Tomorrow's a big day for Christmas. Christmas the town, that is. There are events all day, including an appearance by Santa. My dad's downstairs trying on the costume. I'll be working part of the time—we usually sell a few trees. But no one misses the Parade of Lights." Her head tilted forward. "Have you heard of it?"

"Someone said something."

"Want to go with me?"

"With you?"

"Well, all of us, really."

"Oh. Yeah, that sounds okay."

Merry grinned. "I thought I'd ask you before Noelle. She has a little crush."

"What'll her boyfriend say about that?"

"He knows how she is. You met him already—Jeff, the guy who works at the tree lot."

"Ah, a hometown boyfriend."

"It's sort of a family tradition. My parents were neighbors who got married when they were eighteen. Nicky and Shannon were high school sweethearts. Jeff and Noelle have been dating since the eighth grade. Now that she's in college, she says she needs to explore other options, but she always comes back to Jeff. He's a patient guy."

"What happened with you?"

She shrugged. "None of my high school boy-friends took. I had my sights set farther afield."

"How far—to Chicago?"

She blinked. "Beyond that."

He couldn't resist any longer; he had to approach her. To touch her. She looked rosy and slightly plump with her shirt buttons gaping over the roundness of her belly.

"To the stars?" he whispered, sliding a palm over her silky hair.

Her lips gathered in a sexy pout. "Maybe."

He wanted to kiss her. But he knew he shouldn't, not without a plan. Serious intent, at the least. An honorable man didn't go around kissing pregnant women on whims.

He pecked her forehead. Pressed an arm around her shoulders. "Let's go downstairs," he suggested, as lightly as possible given that their mutual disappointment had soured the air.

CHAPTER SIX

"Yo, Mom," Cory Marshak hollered from one end of a run-down frame house on Winterberry Street. "That weird writer guy is headed this way."

"What did you say?" Jackie screeched over the ear-piercing shrill of the smoke alarm. A haze hung near the kitchen ceiling. The entire first floor stunk from an apple pie that had bubbled over in the oven while she'd worked on the Capuanos' ancient VCR player. Their grandchild had shoved a PB&J into the cassette slot and they wanted it cleaned out. Lucille Capuano had too big a collection of garage-sale videocassettes to move on, technology-wise. Typical of Jackie's clients, but she liked that they hadn't bought in to the demands of a throwaway society, even if that was only because they were too cheap.

The doorbell rang. With a vivid curse word, Jackie dropped the smoking pie on the counter. The edge of the crust was burnt to a black crisp.

"Someone get the door," she yelled to her sons, who'd discovered Stanley Struck's retro Atari game and hooked it up to the Beechers' old TV. She grabbed a broom with her oven-mitt clad hands and slapped at the button on the alarm until the cover sprang off and the battery shot across the linoleum.

Blessed silence.

Except for the *plink-plonk* of Donkey Kong, the peal of the doorbell and the constant bark of the dog next door.

Jackie stomped to the front door. There was only one weird writer guy in town. Oliver Randall had never stepped foot in her house before, but maybe he had a busted toaster oven.

She threw open the door, determined not to be tongue-tied. "Hey, Ol."

Bewilderment crossed Oliver's face, as if he had no idea who "Ol" might be. Or it might have been her getup that flummoxed him—booties the texture and color of the Cookie Monster, soiled canvas work apron and Flintstones oven mitts. Jackie had once been told she'd look like Betty Rubble, if she'd put on a pelt, heels, rock jewelry and tie a ribbon in her black curls.

Heels? Jewelry? Ribbon? Never gonna happen.

Still, the comparison had tickled her. She'd conveniently forgotten that the line had come from her first louse of a husband, who'd wanted to get into her pants at the time. Cartoon references were the height of his complimentary possibilities.

"Uh," Oliver said. "Hello."

"Jackie." She pointed one of the oven mitts at herself. "That's my name."

He flushed to the roots of his receding hairline. "I know."

She remembered when Oliver had moved to town, around fifteen years ago. He'd seemed so dashing and exotic to her then, being a man who actually made a living by writing down stories he made up in his head. Jackie couldn't comprehend having that much imagination. But then she'd been only eighteen, a newlywed dealing with two kids—one in diapers and one who wouldn't hoist his cartoon-watching butt off the couch to look for a job. Her life view had been pretty darn limited.

Some things never changed.

"What can I do for ya?" She took off the mitts and flapped them at the smoke that had drifted toward the open door. "Come in, first. Close the door. I can't afford to heat the neighborhood."

She didn't know why she was being so gruff, when Oliver already looked wary enough to bolt. Maybe it was that she was miffed because, in all these years, he'd never once looked her way. She was invisible to him, even when his beloved Meredith York had been two states away and living with another man.

Oliver jabbed his hands into the pockets of his coat. "Meredith said I should come over."

"Yeah?"

"I'm, um, looking for a murder method."

Jackie cackled. Writers were weird, all right. "Then you came to the right place. I've done away with two husbands." She looked him up and down. "So far."

Oliver shrank back. "What?"

"In my head," she said. "I'm not actually offing them 'til I get the child support I'm owed. Do you want some pie? It's burned, but I can break off the black parts."

"Well, I…"

"I promise, it's still edible. Just not up to York standards, y'know?" She walked to the kitchen, expecting him to follow. Which he did, after a couple of seconds of goggling after her.

She windmilled at the smoke. "Have a seat. I was gonna bring the pie to Christmas dinner, but I guess I'll have to make something else."

"You're going to the Yorks'?" Oliver's worried frown smoothed out. "Me, too."

"Sure, all of us gooseberries are invited." Jackie poked at the offending dessert. She'd been born and raised in Christmas, but her mom had moved on long ago. "Shoot. The pie's too hot to cut."

"That's okay." Clearly relieved, Oliver sat at the table and gave the humble kitchen a quick scan. With the stained ceramic sink, late 70s appliances and ancient wallpaper above the beadboard panel chair rail, it wasn't exactly showroom ready. "I'm not hungry."

WWGYD? Jackie wondered. *What would Grace*

York do? The woman was the town authority on gracious living. Merry turning up unmarried and pregnant had put only a minor black mark on her mother's record.

"I can give you coffee and store-bought Christmas cookies," Jackie offered. "If my boys didn't eat them all."

Merry and Mike had looked so cozy yesterday, over their plate of cookies. But Jackie knew she wasn't the kind of woman who could pull that off. Romance to her meant beer and backseats.

Romance? Hell. Oliver had written the book on it. Several of them, in fact.

She got him a cup, tossed a couple of cookies on a plate and plunked them on the table. While Oliver added two heaping spoons of sugar, she leaned against the Formica counter. "I hear you're working on a new book."

"That's right."

"A romantic suspense?" she asked hopefully. She'd read them all, but she liked the romances best.

"A mystery. Merry said you might have an idea of how I could kill a character, using, uh, a household appliance. Something unusual, but not too far out."

Oliver stopped, having uttered the most words Jackie had ever heard him speak at one time. He tugged on his collar. She watched his Adam's apple bob. He was nervous? Talking to *her?*

She'd never made a man nervous before.

She preened for about five seconds, until she remembered that talking to *anyone* made Oliver nervous. He carried on great conversations with himself, though. She'd seen him jabbering during his long walks in the countryside and had wished that just once there'd be a man who'd talk to her like that. Especially if he didn't expect anything from her other than listening.

Instead, she'd wound up married to Lunkhead One and Lunkhead Two, who thought conversation was for pussies and books for pansies. Hubby number two had complained bitterly about her wasting money on books and had once tossed a pile of them into the fireplace during a fight, even though she usually got them from the library or paid a quarter a pop at the used bookstore.

After that, she'd kicked him out. No one messed with Jackie Marshak's books. She hadn't grown up as a reader, but fiction had frequently been her only refuge as an adult.

Oliver was still stirring. "What do you think?"

"Murder," she mused. "How about electrocution by toaster?"

He nodded. "Along those lines. But, you know, more unique."

"Sure, I can help. Want to see my workroom?" Without waiting for his response, she headed back in the other direction, to the front room she'd turned in to the work space for her freelance business fixing large and small electrical appliances. Lucky for her, there were a lot of penny-pinchers in town who didn't believe in trashing a blender that wouldn't puree or a microwave that had quit nuking. She also collected junked items and broke them down for parts.

"Boys!" she bellowed. "Put down the joysticks and go take a hike." She glanced at Oliver, who was trailing her like a sad-sack basset hound. "Or, y'know, read a book."

Her sons, Jimmy and Cory, the grumpy teenager and the curious ten-year-old, respectively, said mumbling hellos and scrambled out of the room. Oliver looked after them with a bemused expression.

When he turned back, Jackie met his eyes, and for once Oliver didn't immediately back away. He actually studied her, and not as if she were a frog splayed open in biology class, either.

That made her feel odd, so she cast about for distraction, finding plenty in the oily flotsam and jetsam of her work bench. Her gaze lighted on an old radio, which she'd picked out of the dump, then fixed up so she could play music while she worked. NPR was her favorite, but she switched to an oldies rock station whenever they got too talky and highfalutin.

"Hey, Ol," she ventured, following some long-submerged female instinct to sweep off the frowsy bandanna she wore to keep her hair out of her eyes while she worked. She gave the bouncy curls a shake. "You ever hear of solenoid poisoning?"

"HOW DO YOU GET AWAY from home without packing a spare tire around the gut?" Mike asked, hefting an ax in his hand. There'd been pancakes for breakfast. Grace hadn't stopped shoveling them onto Mike's plate until he'd eaten six of them. Plus a thick slice of ham and a tall glass of Merry's cranberry fizz.

"Hard work." Nicky settled three freshly cut lengths of log over his son's extended arms. Skip marched them to the woodpile by the back door of the farmhouse. "Firewood is always good for working up a good sweat."

Mike set a heavy chunk of aged oak on the chopping block. "My pores are oozing maple syrup instead."

Nicky's teeth flashed in the sunshine. "Yeah, I think Merry's sweet on you, too."

"Cute." Mike eyed the wood, raised the ax high overhead and swung it down with a satisfying crack. The split pieces fell to the trampled snow. "How come you never said she's—" He glanced at the boys. "Expecting?"

"That means pregnant," Skip told Georgie, over near the woodpile.

"I guess it didn't occur to me." Nicky raised his brows. "I didn't figure you'd fall in love at first sight—and *then* notice what you should have seen right off."

"Shut up, man." Mike flicked his head toward the boys, then split several more logs before adding below his breath, "I'm not in love."

"Don't resist the inevitable," Nicky teased. "She's a great girl."

"Why is it that I never met her before?" Wishing was a waste of time, but Mike couldn't help wondering what might have been. "Didn't she ever come for a visit?"

"She did, but it must have been when you were assigned elsewhere. Anyway, she brought her boyfriend. Greg Conner…Conway…Clownman, something like that."

Mike swung. The ax got stuck in a stubborn log and he banged it against the block until it split with a cracking noise. He pushed the pieces into the growing pile and took a breather, mopping his face with the back of his pitchy glove. "What was he like?"

Nicky gathered wood. His sons had wandered off to follow a squirrel that had dived into a snowdrift and then popped up several feet away. "He was some sort of executive in the same finance company where Merry worked. An okay guy, but too impressed with himself. He did a lot of bragging and charmed the ladies with pretty-ass compliments."

"Uh-huh."

"We played golf, I remember. Greg had an eye for other women, and a loose tongue, but he kept it under wraps as soon as he saw I wasn't going to play along." Nicky dropped off an armful of logs. "You know I'm no prude, but jeez, when a man is with my sister I don't want to hear comments about their sex life."

The reflection off the snow was glaring. Mike squinted. "Good or bad comments?"

Nicky slapped his gloves against his legs. "Hell, I don't know."

"Why'd they break up?"

"For a man who's not in love, you're asking a lot of questions."

"I'm interested, that's all," Mike conceded.

For a second, he thought Nicky would make another quip. He didn't, turning serious as he lowered his voice. "Merry hasn't said much to me, but according to Shannon, Greg cheated on her. When she found out and told him to leave, he begged for another chance, but Mer's not easy to persuade. Once she makes up her mind…" Nicky executed a slicing motion across his throat.

Something to remember. Mike made a mental note not to play games with consequences he wasn't ready to handle. That included leading a pregnant woman to believe in him. Ever since his father's death, he'd known what a burden accountability could be.

Nicky glanced at his sons, who were now packing

snowballs. "Heads up, Cappy. We've got incoming missiles. Five, four, three, two—"

The first snowball hit Nicky in the left shoulder. He released a theatrical cry of pain and staggered toward the closest snowdrift.

The second, lobbed by Georgie, nailed Mike when he made a leap into its path, masquerading the move as a dodge.

"We got 'em!" Georgie yelled.

Skip's fist pumped the air. "Charge!"

"Man up, Captain America. This is war." Nicky scooped snow and lobbed it at the boys. Mike joined in, ducking as the boys relentlessly pelted them from their store of ammunition.

For ten minutes, the frozen missiles flew back and forth, until they were all clotted with snow and gasping for breath. They were about to quit when Shannon and Merry rounded the corner of the farmhouse.

"Boys, it's time to get ready for town," Shannon said. She stopped when she saw them, ruddy-cheeked and panting. She thrust Kathlyn into Merry's arms. "Run. Save the baby. We've stumbled onto a battlefield."

Skip and Georgie let out whoops of delight and began lobbing snowballs at their mother, while Merry ducked back the way she'd come, clutching the snowsuited baby to her chest.

Mike packed a nice round snowball and crept

around the other side of the house, leaving the gleeful shouts behind. Merry stood near the front porch, jogging the chubby little girl in her arm, talking to her in burbles and coos.

When she caught sight of him, he straightened, holding the snowball behind his back as he sauntered toward them.

Merry turned. "Look, Kathlyn, it's the abominable snowman." The little girl smiled widely and gurgled nonsense sounds, waving her hands at Mike. Merry remained dubious. "What have you got in your hand?"

"Nothing."

"Just a snowball?"

He held it up. "That was my first snowball fight. Would you begrudge a neophyte an easy target?"

Merry tilted her head toward the war cries of Nicky's family. "Go play with the other children. I'm holding a baby."

"But I wanna play with you."

Her eyes widened. He couldn't get over his fascination with how blue they were, especially with her pupils shrunk to tiny dots. Nicky's little girl had big blue eyes, too, but with soft brown hair that curled around her pink cheeks. For a moment, he imagined that Kathlyn was Merry's child.

His and Merry's.

Crazy. He took the snowball and smashed it on top of his own head.

Merry gaped. "You're nuts, Michael Kavanaugh!"

"What's a little more snow? I've already got it all down my collar and up my sleeves." He shook his head, sending bits of the cold stuff flying.

Specks landed on Merry and Kathlyn. The little girl shrieked and giggled. "That's cold, isn't it, baby?" Merry dabbed at her niece's face and gave her a hug.

Mike made a move as if he meant to nuzzle them both with his snow-laden head. He landed a peck on the baby's cheek instead, surprising himself by the affectionate gesture. Little boys he understood, but girls?

Even big girls could be confounding. He glanced at Merry, who'd caught her bottom lip between her teeth. Damn, but he wanted to kiss her, too, no matter how many times he told himself that was the wrong way to go for a man who took his responsibilities so seriously that he avoided those that weren't absolutely necessary.

He touched his thumb to her chin, wiping away a cold trickle. "You're melting."

She said nothing, but was leaning toward him when the Yorks trooped around the corner.

Merry pulled back, hoisting Kathlyn higher in her embrace. "C'mon, sweetie. Let's get away from these crazy people."

"You're coming to town with us?" Mike asked as they all brushed off on the porch.

Merry stopped at the door. "I'll be there, but I have to stop off at the tree lot first to check that we're all set. I'll see you around."

"Remember, we have a date for that parade thing."

She fussed with Kathlyn's furry pink muffler. "Oh, so now it's a date?"

"Yes, and don't forget that *you* did the asking."

A festive appreciation danced in her eyes. "Well, then. Merry Christmas to me."

He grinned. "I think that's my line."

If he got his holiday wish.

THE ENTIRE TOWN TURNED OUT for the Christmas festival, put on two days before the actual holiday. Tourists and citizens from local villages tripled the attendance. Every area business was packed. There were waiting lines to get into the town's only restaurants, a diner and a Swiss chalet called the Matterhorn Inn. As the festivities continued into the late afternoon, the Christmas Cheer became even more popular. Hot toddies, mulled wine, hard cider and peppermint schnapps were served.

Merry had hired extra workers to keep Evergreen and the tree lot open, plus set up a booth at the center of town. She worked there beside Jackie, while Noelle and Jeff handled the final tree sales of the year.

Every time Merry turned around, Mike was nearby, doing what he could to help out, even though she would then banish him to participate in the dogsled rides or the Christmas cookie eating contest.

As the day wore on, she noticed that he'd made a few friends. He was recruited to judge the children's snow angels art display in the town hall, then roped into substituting for a horn player in the town band. She hadn't even known he could play.

By late afternoon, Merry closed up the booth to give her employees the remainder of the day to enjoy the festival. With Mike still tootling in the band, she went to get warm at the Methodist church, where a cake walk was gearing up. She sat back and enjoyed the scramble as the culinary musical chairs proceeded, with her father doing his best to win the most coveted prize of all—Grace York's ginger mascarpone coconut icebox cake.

Santa's arrival capped the day's events. They had no reindeer, so Saint Nick arrived in a sleigh pulled by a pair of horses. It was quite a spectacle, with sleigh bells ringing and Santa ho-hoing as the sled pulled up in the center of town. Clamoring children gathered around. Even the skeptical ones, like Skip, looked as if they'd been struck by the magic and spirit of the season.

Merry was among the audience that had gathered to watch the jolly Santa and his Mrs. Claus distribute candy and small gifts from the back of the sleigh. Mike sidled through the crowd to stand beside her. He put an arm around her. Judging by her tingling reaction, there was more than Christmas magic in the air.

She nudged him. "Are you enjoying your first Christmas festival?"

"I've never seen anything like it."

"Is that good?"

He nodded, smiling as Georgie ran to his parents, excited over the decidedly low-tech rubber-band airplane he'd received even though his Christmas gift list was packed with electronic gadgets. "It's a good old-fashioned time. I didn't think that people still did that."

"In small towns, you have to make your own fun." Mike's arm felt so good around her that she wanted to snuggle with him, but was too aware of the interest they were receiving from a few local ladies. "Some of the events have changed over the years, but my father's been Santa Claus for as long as I can remember. I used to climb up on the sleigh to help him out." She laughed. "I felt so privileged."

"I can see you—a cute little blond Christmas angel."

"Hah. They made me wear an elf costume. By the time I was twelve, I wouldn't be caught dead near my hokey Mr. and Mrs. Claus parents."

"Just think, next year, your baby will be participating."

Merry's emotions welled. "That seems remarkable, but I don't know why. I went to school with the parents of lots of these kids." She smiled at Mike, blinking to keep the tears back. "All part of the circle of life, right?"

He hugged her closer.

She put her mitten to her nose and sniffed. "Good grief. Must be the hormones."

"Don't fob it off on hormones. You're entitled to feel emotional."

She sighed. "But I'm not usually like this."

"That's too bad." He put his cheek near hers. "I think it's nice."

The gift distribution had wound up. The crowd dispersed, some heading off to get warm, while others staked out their spots along the main street parade route.

"What happens next?" Mike asked as they walked over to join Nicky's family. Santa and Mrs. Claus were waving from the back of the sled as they pulled out of town.

"The parade," Shannon said. "We've got about forty-five minutes before it begins. Not enough time to go home and warm up." She put her bare hands over her son's mottled cheeks. "I think Georgie is on the verge of frost bite." In her father's arms, Kathlyn was wrapped like a papoose.

"Hey, gang!" Jackie waved from across the street. She scurried over to join them, her petite frame enveloped by the large khaki parka. She peered out from the fur-lined hood. "Why don't you come to my house to warm up, if you don't mind sharing space with four broken vacuum cleaners and a gutted TV?"

They agreed that was a good plan and headed over to the Marshaks' house. Once there, Jackie cornered Shannon and Merry in the kitchen. "Guess who came to visit?" She didn't wait for their answers. "Oliver Randall."

Merry was pleased to see Jackie's excitement. "What did he want?"

Jackie dumped old coffee into the sink and rinsed the carafe. "Like you don't know, Miss Meredith Matchmaker. Were you trying to set us up, or what?"

"I may have nudged him in the right direction."

"But he likes you. He's always liked you."

There was no use denying that. "His devotion has been impressive, though misplaced." Merry handed her friend a coffee filter. "You know that I'm not interested in Oliver. I never have been."

Jackie's eyes narrowed. "How come?" she asked in a hurt tone. "What's wrong with him?"

"Nothing's *wrong*. It's a matter of…" Merry lifted her hands. "Chemistry."

Jackie finished setting up the coffee machine while her old oil burner furnace roared from the basement, sending delicious warmth through the floor vents. Outdoors, the daylight waned. At the center of town, the decorated Christmas tree that was the town's answer to Rockefeller Plaza began to glow more vividly, its halo of colored light becoming visible past the frost-rimmed kitchen window, beyond the neighboring homes.

"I don't know if I have chemistry with Ol," Jackie ventured, almost shyly, as the coffee began to perk. "He doesn't get close enough for me to find out."

"Some guys," Shannon said, "have to be hit over the head before they notice you." Her gaze slid to Merry. "Others notice you right off, but they're skittish."

Skittish was not the word Merry would have used to describe Mike. Resistant, maybe, and not even that, most of the time.

She reached for the mug Jackie handed her, almost letting it slip from her grasp when another meaning occurred to her. Was Shannon referring to *Merry* as skittish?

And did that fit?

She certainly had reason. Her pregnancy wasn't merely a complicating factor. It was big. Life-changing. More important than anything else, even Mike.

"I asked Oliver to the parade," Jackie confessed as they carried the mugs of hot coffee into the next room for the men. "He didn't really answer. I don't know if he'll show up or not."

"That's fantastic." Merry grinned. She loved it when a matchmaking plan came together. "I mean, that you asked him. Good for you."

Jackie shrugged negligently. "We were talking the ways and means of murder, so it wasn't one of your all-time great romantic moments."

The adults gulped down the coffee and bundled up the kids again, who were eager to stake out a prime viewing spot for the parade. Merry linked arms with Georgie and Skip as they hurried back to the center of town, but before long she found herself standing beside Mike once more. He had a way of always being at hand. Having someone to count on was becoming familiar to Merry. And awfully nice.

Georgie had danced out into the street and hunkered down to study the darkened distance. "I see it, I see the lights!" he called. "Here comes the parade."

Mike took Merry's hand and squeezed it. "Thanks for sharing this with me."

"Anytime." She searched for something sweet to say that wouldn't turn as sappy as she was feeling. "I'm glad you came home with Nicky."

"Home?" He reflected, the light in his eyes turning them from hazel to amber. "Yeah. This is a good place to call home. I'm starting to understand why you returned."

"Call me sentimental, but I'd always believed the saying that home is where the heart is." She rocked on her heels. The excitement in the air was catching. "Now I know that my heart belongs in Christmas."

CHAPTER SEVEN

MIKE WASN'T SURE what he'd expected of the Parade of Lights, but he'd guessed that it wouldn't be like a big city parade. And it certainly wasn't. For the most part, the homespun procession was made up of pickups strung with lights and garlands, with a lot of cheering, hooting and hollering by drunken revelers.

A middle-aged male drill squad passed by in Santa hats with blinking rope lights looped around their necks. At intervals, they stopped and did a choreographed snow-shovel street ballet. Next came a couple of flatbed trailers made up like floats, with flocked Christmas trees and lawn decorations. The town band marched past, playing classic Christmas songs. They were followed by the horse-drawn sleigh carrying the Yorks in their Santa and Mrs. Claus getups.

Mike found himself smiling more than he had in months. The entire day had been slightly surreal, with its simple pleasures and retro hometown vibe. Nicky had warned him that life was different in Christmas, but experiencing it firsthand had really brought the point home.

While he couldn't imagine living here, he understood the appeal. Particularly to Merry.

She glanced at him, so flushed and pretty in the cold wintry air that for a couple of seconds he felt weak at the knees. "Look at Georgie," she said. "Isn't he cute?"

The boy was perched atop his father's shoulders for a better vantage point. He took in the parade with awed eyes, thoroughly entranced by the spectacle. Skip was trying to act more grown-up, but Mike could see that he felt a little left out, squeezed in among too many adults.

He ducked down. "Climb aboard."

"Nah."

"Come on." Mike cuffed the boy on the shoulder. "You're missing too much from down here."

Skip clambered onto Mike's shoulders and he straightened, keeping a good hold on the boy's skinny legs.

Merry's approving glance felt like a reward. She looked down the street and waved. "Here come Noelle and Jeff."

They were in the bed of a red pickup truck emblazoned with the York Tree Farm logo. The sides had been decked out in blinking strings of light and flashy gold garlands. A boom box played "A Rockin' Christmas Eve" while they tossed candy canes to the crowd.

Noelle saw them and waved wildly. She pitched a handful of the candy. "Skip, Georgie! Catch!"

Skip threw himself forward to grab one of the flying candy canes. Mike just managed to keep his balance.

Soon afterward, the parade petered out with a ragtag group bringing up the rear guard. A dozen men in hunter's blaze orange and Elmer Fudd caps pushed lit-up snowblowers, which sent geysers of snow out across the crowd. Amid laughter over the dousing, the spectators broke up, hurrying off to the warmth of their cars.

The Yorks gathered and walked as a group toward their vehicles. "Yoo-hoo," Jackie called from the other side of the street. "Great parade, huh?" She made a pop-eyed face at Merry and pointed at the man beside her. He was tall and lanky, with a knit stocking cap pulled down to the rim of his glasses.

"That's Oliver Randall," Merry said, when she noticed Mike looking. .

"Ah, the famous writer." With the equally famous crush on Merry.

Displaying an air of satisfaction, she nodded. "That's him. It looks like they're getting along."

They reached the cars. Mike lowered Skip to the ground. Georgie was already half asleep, a candy cane hanging out of the corner of his mouth. Nicky set him in the backseat of their minivan while his wife buckled their daughter into a car seat.

"We'll wait for Mom and Dad," Shannon said with

a significant look at Merry. "They should be along any minute. But you two go ahead."

Not too obvious, Mike thought, though he wasn't complaining. They said goodbye.

"I'm done in. Going straight home." Merry fiddled with the fringe of her cashmere scarf as Mike followed her to the Jeep. "You're welcome to come over, if you don't mind a casual evening at home."

"Sounds good." He could use the downtime. That he would be alone with Merry was pure bonus.

"They were all smiling at you, you know," she said once they were settled in the Jeep. It was ice cold. "My family, of course, but everyone else, too." She started the engine and flicked the heater on high. "Brr."

"Smiling at me? I thought it was my natural charm."

"Smiling as in wink, wink, nudge, nudge." She rubbed her hands. "Didn't you notice the looks we were getting all day, whenever we came within two feet of each other? Even private business is public in a small town like Christmas."

"I'm not attuned to the subtleties of the local townsfolk. Does the attention bother you?"

"I'm used to it, but somehow, it's different now, considering my pregnancy. They're looking to marry me off—especially my mother's cronies. I'm surprised that my aunt Adele didn't collar you for an interrogation. Or did she?"

"Uh, no. I don't think so."

She chuckled. "Trust me, you'd know if she had. Just wait till Christmas dinner. Army tanks have nothing on Aunt Adele."

She'd made a joke, but he couldn't laugh. He was still trying to get used to her using the word *marry*. If that's what was at stake…

If? He'd known all along that it was. He just hadn't acknowledged it so openly, even to himself.

Time to wake up, before he found himself cooked like a Christmas goose.

MERRY'S HOUSE WAS SMALL, even to a man who'd spent six months of the past year bunking in a compact ship berth. The house was also comfortable, with a cushy love seat and armchair, and pleasantly warm. Coming after the vigorous outdoor air, the heat had him drifting off into a haze of domestic satisfaction in no time.

Wake up.

Merry came into the room with a glass of mulled red wine for him and hot chocolate for her. She set them on the coffee table and dropped into the chair. With a sigh, she eased into a comfortable position. "Hey, you. Don't fall asleep on me. I put a seafood pilaf casserole in the oven. Just leftovers. I hope you're hungry."

"I ate two pasties," he said, speaking of the U.P. favorite, a meat-and-potato pie enclosed in crust. "And three of those prune things."

"Tarts."

"I never knew prunes could taste so good." He gave her an approving look, his thoughts occupied with more than pastry.

She'd brushed out her hair and changed her clothes, put on a fleece pullover and some kind of loose, soft pants, with plush slippers on her feet. Her expression was dreamy as she idly rubbed her middle with a circular motion.

He looked away, crossing his arms behind his head and knocking together his stocking-clad feet. He yawned. "I feel like a bear in winter hibernation. Totally knocked out."

"Two pasties and three tarts will do that to you."

"Give me a kick if I start snoring."

She picked up a pillow and tucked it behind her neck. "There's nothing that'll knock you out like a day outdoors in the cold. Nicky and I used to play for hours, making snow forts or sledding on the town hill. We'd come home with chapped lips and frozen noses, then nod off into our dinner plates."

"What about Noelle?"

"She wasn't even born yet. Mom calls her a change of life baby. It caused quite the furor when she announced the pregnancy. Nicky and I were both teenagers and terribly embarrassed that our parents were still having marital relations, as Mom called it." She smiled fondly at the memory and patted her stomach. "I guess I'm getting her back now."

"Your childhood seems idyllic."

"I don't have any complaints."

"Is that why you came home, to give your baby the same? Because a few times I've sensed that you've outgrown Christmas."

Sadness tinged her smile. "Does anyone ever get too old for Christmas?"

He sat forward and took a sip of the warm, fragrant wine. "You know what I mean."

"Sure," she said, but she didn't respond beyond that.

He settled back again, noticing that she'd switched on a CD player. Classical music played softly in the background. An idyllic evening, except that he wanted to feel Merry beside him, snuggled up close.

He didn't know why his reaction to her had been so strong from the start. The easy explanation was that any man would crave home and hearth, coming off one deployment and soon to face another. Yet he knew his feelings went deeper than that.

Simply put, she not only excited his interest, she tugged at his heart.

Was it because of her pregnancy, that she needed a partner, a…oh, hell, why not come out with it even though she'd probably protest—a protector?

He'd made few commitments in the past decade. The Navy was paramount, while his engagement to Denise had taken a distant second place. If he looked at that choice nakedly, he could admit that he'd asked her in the first place because it had been easy. Uncomplicated. He'd risked very little. No wonder they'd drifted apart.

"A mother will do anything for her child," Merry said at last. "It's not as if I don't love the town. I can have a very good life here."

"You'll feel restrained."

She flicked a hand. "There are worse things."

Why was he pushing? *Let her be. Unless you're ready to step up, let her live her own life.*

"I'd better get that casserole out of the oven," she said, rising and stepping past his extended legs.

He sat up and caught her around the waist, pulling her down beside him on the love seat. She let out a sound of surprise that softened into a purr as their bodies melded.

"I've been wanting to do this all day," he whispered into her hair. He kissed and stroked it, working his way around to her lips.

"Good thing you didn't. We really would've given the gossips something to talk about."

They kissed. He'd thought that their kiss on the porch that first night had been special, but this was even better, finally holding Merry in his arms, feeling the warmth and softness of her as her lips and tongue moved against his.

Knowing that the kisses weren't leading to the next step, but were only about their pleasure in the here and now, he was able to savor every touch and taste and tender but excruciating caress. He cupped the back of her head, tilting her mouth at just the right angle to deepen the next kiss. Then the next. If he had his way, he'd never stop.

But Merry moved restlessly, pressing her leg between his, coming a little too close to his aching erection. He shifted, stroking her thigh, the lush curve of her hip.

She shivered as he put a hand under her shirt, sliding his palm over the ripeness of her belly. Her skin was hot and cold at the same time. And so incredibly smooth. He grazed her breasts, only briefly, too stricken by the intensity of his spiking desire to continue. Heat roared through him like afterburn exhaust.

He tugged her top back into place and pushed away, putting a couple of inches between them. His pulse was going like gangbusters.

"You're confusing me." Merry brushed her hair back from her flushed cheeks.

"I'm confusing myself."

"There have been a few mixed signals."

"I know. I'm sorry."

"It's okay. I understand. I'm not sure what I'm doing, either, except that—" She stopped, her eyes huge as they stared into his for an unblinking moment. With a sexy curve of a smile, she leaned in to kiss him. "The truth is, I like being with you. I know you're only here for a week. There's no future in this. But still I can't help being drawn to you. So maybe we can just enjoy the moment, you know?"

She was giving him an out. He breathed a little bit easier.

At the same time, he wondered.

Was an out what he wanted?

WITH THE FESTIVAL OVER and the tree lot shut down for the remainder of the season, Christmas Eve day was the family's time to relax and take care of their final preparations for the next day. By midmorning, the women had gathered in the kitchen for the final cookie baking while Grace and Charlie went to the Matterhorn Inn for its well-attended brunch buffet.

Merry unwrapped a stick of butter and dropped it into a saucepan. Shannon started rolling out the dough for a fresh batch of tarts. Noelle wasn't into baking, but she was willing to supervise.

"What's wrong with this picture?" she said from her perch on a stool. "The men are all out snowmobiling while we womenfolk labor in the kitchen."

Merry handed her sister a bag of walnuts and a knife. "Here's some labor for you. I need one cup, chopped, for the church window cookies."

"I'd rather be baking any day," Shannon said with a toss of her head. She sprinkled flour on the butcher block, humming beneath her breath. Although she'd earned a paycheck during the early years of her marriage to Nicky, since the boys had been born she'd lived her dream of being a stay-at-home mom.

At times, Merry found herself envying her sister-in-law's content, perhaps because she didn't expect to be quite such a dedicated mother, at least not to the point where she gave up her career. Shannon had said she'd feel differently once the baby arrived, that Merry would look into its sweet little face and fall in love.

"Baking? Yech. Not me." Noelle ripped open the bag with her teeth and spit out the curl of plastic. "I feel the need, the need for speed."

Merry and Shannon groaned. The *Top Gun* quote was much too familiar around the York household. Even Skip and Georgie used it.

"No, no, No-no." Merry pointed. "Do me a favor and put your energy toward chopping those walnuts—nine hundred nuts per hour, if that makes you happy."

Noelle chopped, but she was not suppressed. "Mike's adorable, don't you think, Shannon? I wonder if he'd go for a younger woman."

Shannon laughed and shook the rolling pin at her. "No, no, No-no." There was a reason the boys had given their young, energetic and occasionally outrageous aunt the nickname.

"Would you two-time Jeff?" The chocolate-and-butter mixture began to melt. Merry stirred with more concentration than strictly necessary.

"We're not exclusive."

"You shouldn't take him for granted. He pines for you when you're gone."

"Pines for me? Hah, that's a good one." Noelle stuck out her tongue. "Gee, I'd better spruce up my attitude, then, huh?"

"I'm not kidding." Merry took the saucepan off the heat. She rummaged in a cupboard for the vanilla. "One of these days, you might come home and find out that Jeff's not waiting for you."

Noelle still didn't look daunted. "Yeah, but I'm too young to settle down."

"I suppose that's true."

"I was twenty when I married Nicky," said Shannon. She'd already managed to get a smudge of flour on her cheek. "I knew he was the one for me from the time I was fifteen."

"Cripes," Noelle said. "That's so claustrophobic."

Merry swept the chopped walnuts into the chocolate. "I think it's romantic."

"Since when are you a romantic?" Noelle waved her arms. "The baby's making you soft. You used to be my hero."

"And I'm not anymore, just because I'm pregnant?"

"Not because of that, exactly. It's just—you know

what I mean. You used to have this cool life in the city, and now you're stuck in Christmas."

"Merry's helping out the family." Good old Shannon, always stalwart and supportive.

Merry thanked her sister-in-law with a smile. "I wanted to come home."

Noelle remained skeptical. "Really?" She shrugged. "What about Mike?"

"What about him?"

"C'mon, Mer. It's obvious that you want his bod. And who could blame you? He's hot."

Shannon giggled. "It's a known fact—pregnant women can get pretty horny, after they're past morning sickness and not yet into the whale stage. Like right where Merry is now."

"Shaddup, you," Merry said, laughing despite her embarrassment. Heat rose to her face.

"Oh, my gosh." Noelle's mouth hung open. "What did you two do last night, tucked up all nice and cozy in your little house?"

"Nothing," Merry insisted. "We had a little bit of dinner and we talked, that's all." She was certain they could read the whole story on her face and she bent over the mixing bowl, folding in a bag of minimarshmallows. "Mike was back here by nine-thirty."

"Good thing, too. Dad was joshing about getting out the shotgun."

"Please. If anyone deserves that, it's not—" Merry cut off the thought so fast she almost bit her tongue.

Noelle became serious. "Mom's not here, Mer. You can say it. We all know who the father is."

The sharp sound of Shannon's inhale cut through the tense silence. She looked at Merry and shrugged. They'd shared enough confidences over the past several months for her to be pretty certain about the identity of the baby's father, even if Merry hadn't come out and said it directly.

"It's easier not to get into that," Merry explained in a low voice. "Greg's out of my life and he'll be staying that way. I don't want Mom to think there's even the faintest chance of us getting together."

They let that thought simmer in silence.

"Well, she likes Mike," Noelle said perkily. "I even heard her telling Aunt Adele that she has hopes for you two."

Oh, God. "Mike is going away in a few days." Merry did a karate chop. "End of story."

"Hey," Shannon protested. She brushed her bangs out of her eyes with the back of her wrist. "It doesn't have to be the end, does it?"

Merry gave her a warning look. "Don't tell me that you have hopes, too."

Shannon wrinkled her nose. "Sorry, but so does Nicky."

"Poor Mike." Trying to keep her mind on the task at hand instead of her love life, Merry ripped out a piece of waxed paper, laid out the cookie mixture in a log shape and added a sprinkling of coconut. "He comes for what should have been a pleasant holiday visit and suddenly finds himself the main player in my baby stakes."

"Whoa," Noelle said. "I was only teasing."

Shannon frowned. "Is he protesting?"

Merry rolled and wrapped the log. "Not exactly. But he's not looking to enlist, either, and I sure don't blame him." She glanced up at the whining buzz of snowmobiles in the distance. "Please, can we table this discussion? It sounds like the guys are heading back this way."

Shannon and Noelle exchanged a look before launching into a comparison of how many gifts they had to wrap for the next morning. Merry moved to the refrigerator and paused there with the door open, letting the air cool her cheeks.

She hadn't started out with a plan to be secretive about the baby's father. It had seemed discreet not to explain how she'd engaged in what was essentially a one-night stand, even if it had been with a man she'd lived with for years. Coming out with an explanation now was only stirring things up.

Or was she just making excuses, because confessing would be more than a tad humiliating?

The phone rang and Noelle went to answer it.

"Take it easy," Shannon murmured over the dough she was stamping with a square cookie cutter. "You look like you swallowed a Christmas turkey."

Merry smiled wryly. "Don't you mean a basket-ball?"

Shannon's head angled back to visually measure Merry's girth. "Nope. You've got a few months to go before you're at basketball stage."

The snowmobiles had pulled up outside. A minute later, the menfolk arrived with a clatter of loud out-door voices and stomping boots. They called hello from the entryway.

Noelle appeared steps ahead of them, the tele-phone receiver at her ear. She waved for quiet, and her expression was so stark that they all obeyed in-stantly, even the excited boys.

"Noelle?" Merry whispered.

Her sister shook her head. "We'll leave right away," she said and lowered the phone. She clutched the receiver under her chin. "Dad started having chest pains while they were at the buffet. He's been sent to the hospital in an ambulance."

Merry stepped back involuntarily, as if she'd taken a punch.

Shannon moaned. "Oh, no."

"Mom?" Georgie quavered.

Nicky scooped him up. "Was it a heart attack?"

"I don't know," Noelle said in a high-pitched voice. "That was Aunt Adele. She was at the buffet when it happened, but she didn't know how bad it was. She said Mom insisted on going in the ambu-lance with Dad."

An eerie echo of the fear that had swept through Merry when she'd gotten the call about her dad's first heart episode returned. She'd felt so helpless back then that she'd thought it would be better to be at hand instead of waiting to hear long distance, but she'd been wrong. Nothing mollified the frightening experience.

"We have to go," she said. "Right away." She spun in a circle, picked up the rolling pin and looked at it curiously.

Mike came forward and gently pried it from her fingers. He wrapped his arms around her. With a breathy sob, she let herself lean on him, knowing that even when the world around her crumbled, she was safe with Mike.

CHAPTER EIGHT

AN HOUR LATER and seventy-five miles away from Christmas, Merry hugged her mother in the hospital corridor. "It's okay, honey," Grace York said, rubbing her daughter between the shoulder blades, as she'd done to all of her children when they were sick or upset. "He's going to be fine."

Noelle and Shannon moved into the embrace.

"Thank heaven," Nicky said.

"It was angina." Grace took a deep, wet breath. "Oh, my. I need to sit down."

They walked her to the seats in the waiting area, crowding around to offer whatever comfort they could, water and coffee or fast, hard-squeezed hugs. She took off her glasses and honked into a tissue.

Merry swallowed. Her mother's face was bare and vulnerable without glasses. And she seemed so small, out of the kitchen and in an unfamiliar location. Soon she'd be old and fragile, perhaps needing her children more than they needed her.

Moving back home was the best thing I ever did.

I'll never complain about Dad's interference or Mom's disapproval again.

Merry dabbed her eyes. Yeah, that sounded good, even if she'd probably stick to the promise as well as she'd kept her vow to go to church every Sunday for the rest of her life if the cutest boy in class asked her to the eighth-grade dance.

"Tell us what happened," Nicky said. He had an arm around his mother and a son in his lap.

Grace set her glasses back in place. "You know how your father loves a buffet. I told him to go easy, but as soon as my back was turned to chat with Adele and Diane—" Grace interrupted herself. "Diane came home for Christmas after all, so I invited her for dinner."

"I doubt if an extra piece of bacon caused this," Shannon said, trying to get Grace back on track.

Behind her lenses, the York matriarch's eyes glinted a steely blue. "Nevertheless. That man is sticking to a heart-healthy menu from here on out."

Merry leaned into Mike's side without even thinking about it. "Which is all well and good, Mom, but what actually happened? What did the doctors say?"

Grace reached over and patted Georgie's cheek. "It was quite the to-do, but we don't have to worry. Grandpa had a few little chest pains and a nice person called for an ambulance. The paramedics gave

Grandpa medicine and he started feeling better almost right away."

"Grandpa rode in an ambulance?" Skip said. "Cool."

Georgie scooted forward. "Wow. Did they play the siren?"

"Indeed they did, and it was terribly loud." Grace covered her ears, keeping a smile on her face for her grandsons' benefit. "But they didn't run it the entire way. Your Grammadear would be deaf if they had."

Nicky put George down. "Okay, Mom. Let's get to it. What have the doctors said?"

"They're certain it was angina. Charlie will have to stay overnight for observation and further tests, but as long as those all check out, he can come home tomorrow. Of course, he'll have to schedule an immediate checkup with his own doctor, but in the meantime, we can still hold our usual Christmas."

"Maybe we shouldn't," Shannon started to say, but her sons' cheers cut her short. She told the boys to hush, reminding them they were in a hospital.

"We will have our Christmas dinner," Grace stated firmly. "It's a tradition."

"But with all this distraction, should we at least scale back? Maybe invite fewer guests," Merry suggested. "I'm sure they'd understand."

"And you don't want to tire Dad out," Noelle put in.

"Nonsense. Your father would think there was

really something wrong with him if we altered our plans." Grace shook her head. "No, Christmas dinner will proceed as usual. Charlie can hold court from his easy chair and I'll keep a close eye on him." She waved. "You girls may be in charge of the dinner, if that makes you any happier."

"Oh, man," Noelle said. "Three of us to replace one of you? I don't like those odds."

A WHILE LATER, they were able to visit Charlie, several of them at a time. Merry approached the bed with trepidation, but her father looked the same as ever, though a little pale and tired.

She kissed his forehead. "Hey, Daddy."

"Meredith." He squeezed her hand. "Lieutenant Commander Kavanaugh."

Mike nodded. "Looking good, sir."

"Pfft. I seem to have turned in to a bionic man."

"It's just an IV and a heart monitor and, um…" Merry watched the beeping machine for a couple of seconds, swearing she could feel her own heart beating in time, stuck halfway up her throat. "Oh, Dad. You gave us a scare. Promise me you'll take better care of yourself."

"Sure, I will," he said. "I plan to be around for a long time, honey. I've got to see that baby of yours grow up and you know there's still all kinds of grief I can give you at the tree lot."

"Anytime," she said in a weepy voice.

Charlie chuckled. "Cripes, don't go soft on me, Mer. You're my best combatant. Arguing with you is good for me. Keeps my blood moving."

The weight pressing on Merry's chest eased a bit. "Okay, Dad. I promise to stick to my guns as hard as ever. As long as you promise to keep firing back."

"You can count on it."

"We'll see you tomorrow." Merry gave his beard a gentle tug. "'Cause we can't have Christmas without our Santa."

"Watch out for your mother. You know how she is about filling up the house and putting on a fancy dinner with all the trimmings. Don't let her overdo."

"Try not to worry. I'm taking charge."

Charlie smiled. "That's my girl."

Merry nodded at the nurse who appeared at the door. "We have to go, Dad."

"Drive safely. I hear they're predicting a blizzard on TV6." Charlie gestured at Mike. "I'm counting on you, too, ace. Take care of this one for me."

Merry leaned down to give him another kiss and whispered, "I take care of myself, Dad."

"Stubborn," he said fondly. "But you'll figure it out. We all need somebody."

Merry withdrew, stealing a glance at Mike before preceding him out the door. The gravity of his expression and the solemn promise in his eyes made her breath catch short. Maybe it was only because her defenses were down and her emotions raw, but she could finally admit the truth.

She did need him.

If only for the few short days they had left.

IT WAS A QUIET Christmas Eve, and surprisingly nice, for all that they missed having Charlie with them. Since nothing was the same, they even managed to persuade Grace that it would be okay to serve takeout pizza for dinner. After they'd eaten and cleared away the paper plates and napkins, she excused herself to go upstairs for a rest before it was time to get ready for the candlelight church service. Some rules might be relaxed, but the Yorks would not miss church.

After a quick call to the hospital to check up on Charlie, Merry put on a CD of Christmas carols and asked Mike to build up the fire in the woodstove. Noelle got the boys interested in helping her do a puzzle, which they spread out on the coffee table.

Nicky sprawled on the couch, intending to nap, but Shannon was in a giggly mood, probably from being overtired. She kept teasing and tickling him. Finally he trapped her in his arms and they both fell back on the couch in a bear hug. Noelle whispered to the boys and they all snickered.

Mike looked up from stirring the fire. Merry felt

his gaze on her. Sparks burst from a knotty chunk of wood in a sizzling, crackling plume. He hurriedly closed the cast-iron door.

"Who wants a game of Scrabble?" she asked brightly.

Shannon nuzzled her husband. "Too much brain strain."

"Noelle?"

"Nope. This puzzle is positively fascinating."

Merry hesitated. "Mike?"

He grinned. "If there's no Xbox around."

"What is it with men and video games? All that violence and speed. There's nothing wrong with a good old-fashioned game of Scrabble or Yahtzee."

"You sound like Mom," Noelle said.

"Nothing wrong with that, either," Merry replied grumpily. She pulled a pillow into her lap.

"I'll play," Mike offered.

"No, there's probably not time before church anyway." Merry put a hand over her mouth and yawned. "I should go upstairs and wrap my last few presents, but I'm too lazy."

"And we have to make milk and cookies for Santa," Georgie said.

Shannon's head lifted off her husband's chest. "Not yet. If we put them out too soon, your dad will just gobble them up before Santa gets here."

Nicky playfully pushed his wife aside and rose up

on one elbow. "Cookies? Did I hear cookies being offered?"

"We want cookies," the boys chorused.

Merry jumped up. "I'll get them."

She was glad to escape. Mike was still looking at her, in that special way that made her scalp tingle and her toes curl. She was certain that she shouldn't be having sexy thoughts, with her father in the hospital and the prospect of putting in a very public church appearance looming on the horizon.

Mike followed her to the kitchen. "How are you doing?"

"Me? I'm fine." She pulled one of the chocolate logs out of the refrigerator and set it on the tile countertop. The waxed paper tore beneath her clumsy fingers.

"You don't have to be fine. Your dad's doing well. You can relax now."

She exhaled. "Right."

"You heard what Charlie said. There's no reason to feel guilty."

Her pent-up anxiety spilled over. "Why did I have to push so hard? He wasn't ready for me to take over. The least I could have done was keep the business the way he liked it."

"But you were making smart changes. You're trying to keep the business thriving."

Her shoulders slumped. "Yeah, I guess so."

"I know." Mike touched her clenched hand, rubbing

his thumb over her knuckles until her fingers slowly uncurled. "Guilt doesn't necessarily listen to logic."

"Why do I always believe you?"

"Because I know what I'm talking about."

She looked closely at him, suddenly remembering a moment in the hospital. He and Nicky had been doing that shoulder-gripping manly hug thing, and she'd thought that it had almost looked as though Mike was the one being consoled.

"What do you mean?" she asked.

He took a few seconds to answer. "My dad died when I was eighteen. Carbon monoxide poisoning from a faulty heater in a vacation cabin."

"How horrible. I'm sorry." She reached for him, stopped, then silently reprimanded herself for being self-conscious about a gesture of affection. "I didn't realize that my dad's situation was affecting you, too," she said, impressed by the quiet, competent way Mike dealt with his issues as they hugged. He was the type of man she wanted in her corner, but she'd also like to give back as much as she received. She and Greg had never been partners that way.

He released her, making a rather sheepish face. "The day brought up a few memories. Nothing for you to worry over."

"That's what family is. People who worry for you."

He cocked his head, giving her that look again. "I'm not family."

"Close enough." She started slicing into the log, creating round flat cookies. "If you haven't figured it out yet, we Yorks have accumulated a big extended family. It's a good thing the population of Christmas is so low, because nearly half the town may be here tomorrow."

Mike watched her arrange the slices on a plate. "Church windows," he said, seeing how the colored marshmallows made a stained-glass pattern in the chocolate. "Now I get it."

"Pure sugar. But Georgie loves them. These need to warm up to room temperature." She took out a plastic storage container the size of a hat box and rummaged through it for a selection of the cookies her mother had been baking and freezing for weeks. Every year, it was a shock how quickly the dozens and dozens of Christmas cookies managed to disappear, although many of them went to church bake sales and neighborhood cookie exchanges even before the Christmas party was held.

Mike hopped up to sit on the counter. "Will you go home after church?"

"No." She tilted her head and smiled at him. "For the next two nights I'll be sharing Noelle's room. The one right next to you."

"Oh." His tone sounded as if he'd meant to say *uh-oh*.

Her pulse accelerated, even though she knew that nothing could happen between them with half a dozen sets of listening ears in the house. "How late do you stay up?"

"As long as it takes."

Her face heated. "Then maybe we'll, mmm, run in to each other in the hall?" She moved between his spread thighs and stretched to drop a light kiss on his lips. He tried to catch hold of her, but she slipped away, and was grateful that she had when her mother entered the kitchen a few seconds later.

Mike instantly slid down off the counter, clearing his throat and generally doing a bad job of looking innocent.

Grace appeared much refreshed. She'd changed into church clothes—a dressy sweater and wool slacks. She took one look at the cookie plate and said, "The boys will never be able to sit quietly for the service if they're all hyped up on sugar."

"Never mind," Shannon said, coming in on her mother-in-law's heels. "I decided the candlelight service will keep them up too long. I'll stay home with them."

Grace's lips crimped with disapproval. "But I wanted us all to go as a family. We're already missing one…" She wasn't above laying on a guilt trip if she had to. "Next thing, I suppose Nicholas will back out."

"He's going." Shannon kept a smile on her face. "I'd like to join you, but I'm sorry, the boys need to stay home."

"I can look after them," Mike volunteered.

"Perfect." Grace bustled into the family room, issuing orders for the room to be picked up and boots and coats to be distributed.

"You're a lifesaver who deserves a cookie." Shannon offered Mike the plate. "Are you sure? The boys are hyper even without sugar. It'll be a challenge to get them in to bed."

He took an almond cookie. "I'll manage."

Merry knew that he would. There didn't seem to be anything he couldn't do well.

Shannon went off to change clothes. Merry nibbled a thumbprint cookie, eyeing Mike. "You're smart to stay home. Appearing with me at the church service would only up the speculation."

"Would that be so terrible?"

"Surely you jest."

"I guess. What I meant was, why do you care so much?"

"Oh, I don't know, maybe because I have to live with my mother's long-suffering sighs?" She laughed to show she wasn't too serious, although there was certainly enough truth to the comment. "I've always been an overachiever. Could be first-child syndrome, I don't know. But this is the first time I've really, truly let down my folks by going against the way they raised us. Well, aside from living in sin with Greg, that is, which at least happened hundreds of miles away so I didn't have to hear about it too often."

Mike's easy expression flickered at the mention of Greg Conway. "This isn't the nineteen-fifties."

"Sometimes it feels like it is, in this town." She considered. "Except you're right. Christmas has its share of reality. There are scandals, affairs, single mothers, petty crime, wife abusers, drugs, alcoholism. And worst of all—litterers."

Mike laughed. "You sure you want to live here?"

She chose to end the conversation on an up note. "Never fear. I'm planning a crusade against the litterers."

AFTER WORKING ON THE PUZZLE, checking over the gifts already under the tree one more time—which involved weighing, shaking and guessing—and leaving cookies and milk on a table near the woodstove, Mike finally persuaded Skip and Georgie to head upstairs to bed. He oversaw pajamas and tooth-brushing, then refereed a debate on how Santa accessed homes without fireplaces. Skip smirked and Georgie became querulous. Mike left them thinking of the constant teasing and tussles he and his younger brother had engaged in, which back then had probably been annoying as hell to their parents, but now seemed merely another aspect of brotherly bonding. He resolved to call his brother and mother the next day and wish them a happy Christmas.

Feeling beat, he went to his third-floor quarters. He

removed his shoes and lined them up under the bed, plumped up the pillows, then swung his legs up and stretched out to wait for Merry.

The moment in the kitchen replayed in his head. She'd be sleeping next door. She'd be looking for him.

What did that mean, precisely?

Even though they were a floor away, he could hear the boys chattering back and forth. Too excited to sleep. Mike smiled, reminded again of the old days. When was the last time he'd felt such anticipation?

Hah. How about right now?

He touched his bristly jaw and thought of shaving. Or would that look presumptuous, as if he expected there to be physical contact?

Cool your jets, ace. If the boys' chat could be heard through the floorboards…

His travel clock read quarter to ten. The Yorks should be home soon.

Mike closed his eyes, summoning up an image of Merry. Yeah, he thought she was beautiful…even pregnant. He wouldn't turn her down if she indicated she was willing.

But the attraction wasn't only physical. Right from the start, he'd been captivated by her style and smarts, her humor and thoughtfulness. At her house the other night, after they'd eaten, then wordlessly agreed to sit a few feet apart so they wouldn't get carried away, they'd talked. Just talked, for more than two hours.

About everything under the sun, from his days as a trumpet-playing band geek, to the corporate career she'd given up and still missed, to their favorites lists for films, books and TV. She went for sweeping epic melodramas, literary fiction and reality shows like *Project Runway* and *Top Chef*. He was all about action and thrillers. Predictable, she'd teased, eventually worming out of him that he'd once watched an entire season of *South Park* on DVD aboard ship.

Headlights flashed at the window. They were home.

Mike vaulted out of bed and grabbed his shaving kit off the bureau. A quick once-over wouldn't hurt.

Downstairs, the Yorks were trying to be quiet, but he heard the murmur of their voices and the *screek* of the door to the woodstove being opened. He ducked into the slant-ceilinged bathroom, hunkering near the mirror to make a quick pass across his jaw with his electric shaver. He brushed his teeth, too, and slipped back to his room as the creaking staircase announced an ascension. Shannon, checking on the boys.

Mike decided not to go down. He'd wait awhile and see if Merry had a plan for them to connect.

Jeesh. He was all nerves and arousal, with not even a sugar rush to blame.

He went to put the kit in the top drawer and noticed the edge of the folded envelope. The Dear John letter. He hadn't thought about it for a couple of days. Maybe it had finally lost its hold on him.

He opened the envelope and scanned the page, trying to figure out why he'd kept it so long.

"We haven't really been in love for a long time now."

True enough.

"You'll take it as a failure, but you shouldn't."

She'd pegged him, there.

He'd blamed himself for neglecting and losing Denise, just as he'd never forgiven himself for not being able to save his father. It wasn't the actual breakup that stung.

It was his failure.

He stood and held the letter over the waste can. Maybe he was finally ready to let the guilt go…all of it.

But not here. He could imagine one of the family emptying the trash and finding the letter.

Better if he took it downstairs and burned it.

The floorboards in the hallway creaked. Mike shoved the letter into the pocket of his jeans and threw open the door.

"Oh. Hey, Noelle."

She was in stocking feet, with her hair curled into an elaborate do, caught up in jeweled clips and hanging halfway down her back. She lit up when she saw Mike. "You're awake."

"Yeah." His gaze strayed to the staircase.

"Mom is making everyone go to bed early, but I'll never be able to sleep yet." She pursed her lips a little, pouting for him, trying to be flirtatious. "Want to meet me downstairs as soon as she's asleep?" She winked. "We can have a nightcap. I'm sure there's some kind of booze in the house."

"Um…"

Noelle wound one of her curls around her finger. "Trust me, this is the only midnight rendezvous on offer. My mother has the ears of a hawk—no, that's the eyes of a hawk, isn't it? What animal has the ears?" She giggled. "Anyway, Merry is way too decent to engage in late-night shenanigans right under her mother's nose. Or above her nose, I guess you'd say. The master bedroom is directly below us."

Of course. He'd been foolish to think otherwise.

"Plus, she gets tired pretty early. You know, 'cause she's pregnant." Noelle smiled. "But not me."

"Well," he said, delaying. "Thanks for the offer, but I'm planning to turn in early, myself. Just wanted to say good-night, is all."

"Sure," Noelle chirped. Her eyes darted like a bird's as her sister appeared in the stairwell.

Merry's gaze was pinned on Mike. "Hi."

"Hi." The word came out all husky, as if it had been stored too long in his throat.

"Dibs on the bathroom," Noelle said before disappearing into her room.

A minute ticked by and Mike could only stare, filling his eyes with the sight of Merry as if it had been years, not mere hours, since he'd seen her last. She was in stocking feet, too. Thick white ankle socks, which looked kind of odd since she'd put on a dress for church. Her boots must be downstairs.

He coughed. "I think your sister was making a move on me."

Merry wrinkled her nose. "Yes, that sounds like Noelle. Were you interested?"

"You're not serious."

"Hey," Noelle said from the bedroom. "I do believe I've been insulted." She laughed.

"No privacy," Merry mouthed, almost silently.

"That's okay." Looking at her was enough.

She shot a glance down the stairs, then put both hands on his chest and pushed him back into the bedroom, following so closely she stepped on his toes. They met in a hasty, clinging embrace, shutting the door with a loud thunk as he propelled her backward against it.

They kissed hungrily.

"I was thinking about this all through the service," she whispered, swallowing a breathy laugh as he kissed her again. "It was wildly improper."

He wanted to never stop kissing her, but somehow he did, holding her face between his hands and turning his aside. He panted. "You'd better go." He grazed his face through her hair, planting little kisses at her temple. "I don't want to get in trouble with Grace and Charlie."

Laughing softly, she slithered out of his arms and opened the door, pausing for just a moment to blow him an air kiss before she slipped away.

He groaned and thumped the door with his fist.

From the next room came Noelle's knowing chortle.

CHAPTER NINE

THE BLIZZARD never arrived, but a picture postcard snow fell in Christmas on Christmas morning. Merry and Mike stood at one of the farmhouse's windows with their coffee, watching the slow drift of flakes from the sky. Beyond the yard, a field stretched in pristine perfection, untouched except by the crisscrossing patterns wild creatures had made during the night.

"I used to take Noelle out when she was a little girl, to identify the tracks. She'd make up stories about the buck who leaped the fence to scare away the fisher who was stalking the snowshoe hare." Merry wrapped her hands around the mug. "Once, we went out at twilight. It was chilly and I wouldn't let her talk, so you can imagine her patience didn't last long. We were about to go in when three deer stepped from the trees into the moonlight. They were incredibly beautiful. I remember every detail to this day."

She looked up at Mike. One side of her mouth quirked. "Is that corny?"

He put his hand between her shoulder blades.

"Nope. Not at all. I saw an elk once, up in the mountains with my dad. Just for a couple of seconds."

"Oh, don't tell me you shot it."

He patted her back. "We were hiking, not hunting."

"Good. Hunting is big up here, but I've never been a venison eater. Noelle, either."

"Wait. You're not a vegetarian, are you?"

She laughed. "Would that be so bad?"

He winked at her and took a sip of coffee.

"Hey, you two dopes," Noelle called from the family room. "Get in here before the boys mow through all the presents without you."

"No-elle," scolded Grace. "I don't like the smart mouth."

Mike and Merry joined the group in the family room, where Nicky was videotaping the morning festivities for Charlie. Skip and Georgie had already had stockings, which they'd opened before breakfast. They'd been up since six.

Soon wrapping paper flew in jagged tears as they dug in to their pile of presents. In between, they helped to distribute gifts to the adults. The loot accumulated quickly, and Mike had to grin at what short work the boys made of the unwrapping, given how much effort the women had put in to finding matching bows and ribbons. He'd laid in bed the past night, listening to Merry and Noelle giggle over their task before heading downstairs with Shannon and

Nicky to set up the artful array that was now a disaster area.

"Thank you, Mike. This is lovely." Merry held up the slender book of poetry she'd unwrapped. He'd found a few gift items during the Christmas festival, including handmade soap and geode coasters for the other women. Selecting presents for females wasn't his talent, but Skip and Georgie were nuts over the electric cars he'd given them.

"Aren't we blessed," Grace said, smiling tearfully at her brood.

Noelle, wearing polka-dot pajamas and a shiny gold bow atop her head, gave her mother a tender kiss. "Grammadear's getting weepy. Time for a rousing chorus of 'Grandma Got Run Over by a Reindeer'."

Soon afterward, Nicky and Mike prepared for the drive to the hospital. It had been decided that Grace would stay home while they made the trip to pick up Charlie and bring him home in time for the Christmas potluck dinner.

Grace fretted over the condition of the roads. "Drive carefully," she said over and over, until Nicky stopped her with a reassuring hug.

"Don't you worry. We'll take good care of Dad. I'll phone you several times to check in, okay?"

A lump had formed in Mike's throat. Christmas in Christmas had unleashed every emotion he'd kept such a tight hold on for so long.

They took snacks—heart-healthy ones—an extra jacket and blankets for Charlie, and double-checked the car's winter emergency kit. Wearing afghans around their shoulders, the woman gathered on the porch to wave goodbye.

"Man," said Nicky as soon as they'd pulled onto the main road in the minivan that had been deemed the safest in potential blizzard conditions. "That was just like going off to war."

The roads were clear and there was little traffic. They made good time, even keeping to the speed limit. Mike watched the barren landscape slide by. Over the past several days, it had grown familiar.

"So how are you holding up?" Nicky asked eventually. "Is the town getting to you yet?"

"That depends. Do you mean in a good way or a bad way?"

Nicky laughed. "Yeah, that's the gist of it."

"I get that the town has its appeals."

Up went an eyebrow.

"Not only Merry." Mike paused. This was dangerous territory to tread, finding the delicate balance between being respectful to his best friend's sister while acknowledging that although he thought she was practically perfect, not to mention smoking hot, he wasn't going to make any promises that couldn't be kept. Most likely, he was going to disappoint her.

Luckily, they avoided the issue for the moment. Nicky started talking about how Shannon had been working on him to decommission when his commitment was up and move back home to pilot commuter planes out of the nearest airport. He was leaning toward giving that a try, mainly because the schedule would give him a lot more time with his kids. "I can always shift direction when they're older," he concluded.

"Sounds like you're heading for the daddy track," Mike observed.

"You'd understand if you had kids. Risky flying lost its attraction real fast when I saw how much Kathlyn has grown up without me."

"I wasn't being critical. I get it."

"She'll be walking before I know it. And talking. I don't want her first words to be, 'Daddy gone bye-bye.'"

They lapsed into a gloomy silence. Mike turned a burning question over in his mind, one he'd been dying to ask but had put off because he wasn't sure he really wanted to know.

Finally, he blurted it out. "Do you know who the father of Merry's baby is?"

"I wondered when you'd get around to that." Nicky glanced away from the road. "Hasn't she told you?"

"Not exactly, but she made a comment. She was kind of riled up. Said something about Greg Conway never being a father to the baby."

Mike gritted his jaw. He'd shoved the statement to the back of his brain, but now he wondered why he hadn't examined it.

No maybes about it. He hadn't wanted to know.

He thrust his head back against the seat. "So that must mean it's Greg, right?"

Nicky made a noncommittal sound. "That's something for Merry to say."

Mike flexed his hands. "Yeah. Okay."

"She's not a game player like a lot of women. She'll be up front with you, if you're up front with her."

Mike didn't know if he could be. He was already entangled enough. Taking the next step, asking her to trust him with the truth about her most precious secret, would only make for more complications.

The kind that might tie them together for good.

THEY COLLECTED Charlie at the hospital in Marquette and drove him safely home, the minivan rocking with music, laughter and the man's never-ending tales. Halfway home, when Nicky tried to get his father to quiet down, Charlie guffawed and said he hadn't busted out of prison to take a nap. He asked for the radio to be cranked up even higher, then launched into a story about driving a truckload of trees to Chicago with bad brakes and two bits in his pocket.

Half an hour later, they arrived safely in Christmas. Charlie insisted he was hale and hearty and raring to go, but Grace whisked him off to the bedroom for a nap. Nicky and Mike claimed they were ready for one, too.

The house hopped with dinner preparations. Mike wandered around feeling useless, until Merry came out and threw herself on the couch. "Oh, my God. I had to get out of that hot kitchen and off my feet. My mother's been driving me crazy. She says we'll run out of food, but we've got enough to feed an army."

Mike lifted her feet off the couch and eased down beside her. "Only a navy."

"Of course." She snuggled into the cushions, lifted her ponytail and rolled her head against the armrest. "Don't touch my feet unless you're serious."

He'd put them in his lap and cupped the heels while working his thumbs over her instep. The conversation with Nicky was still playing over in his mind. He knew now wasn't the time to ask the proverbial sixty-four-thousand-dollar question. Except time was running short. There was only today and tomorrow, and then he was gone.

Right there, that was reason enough not to ask.

But he knew that he had to.

Noelle came in to the family room and threw herself into a chair. "If I never see another lasagna, it'll be too soon. Mom thinks it's healthy because we made it with spinach and low-fat cheese." She perked up when she saw Merry's feet in Mike's lap. "Are you giving free foot massages?" She stuck up a sneakered foot and wiggled it.

"Only to pregnant women," he said.

"Ouch."

Merry pulled her feet away and pulled up into a cross-legged position. "Can we not mention that word? The guests will be probing me with questions all afternoon and evening."

"It's not so bad as that," said Noelle, after she'd snickered at the word *probing*. "You're too sensitive. I'd pay anything to see you stand up to Aunt Adele and all the rest of them. Just stick out your belly and give 'em the big what-for."

"That's what you'd do, not me."

"But you're not a wimp."

Merry frowned. "Do I seem wimpish? I thought I was being discreet, for Mom's sake." She shuddered. "Yuck. I am so sick and tired of this subject."

No one dared to reply, not even Noelle.

Merry's chin jutted. She narrowed her eyes at Mike as if she knew what was on his mind. "For heaven's sake, doesn't anyone realize that I'm more than a pregnancy?"

He still said nothing, although he was thinking plenty. As much as he'd wanted to separate Meredith from her pregnancy, he knew that was impossible. She was a package deal, one that required a full buy-in. Perhaps that description lacked romance, but then so did the practicalities of the situation.

Mike had some hard questions to answer—and he'd better do it soon.

When flying from an aircraft carrier, there was always a point at which he had to turn around before the plane ran out of fuel. He and Merry were rapidly reaching that point of no return.

THE GUESTS BEGAN arriving by late afternoon. The infamous Aunt Adele and her daughter Diane were first. Mike was quickly brought forward for an introduction.

Merry could see that, after the early buildup, he was a little surprised at her aunt's mild appearance. Adele Cozinski was a widow, a plumper version of her younger sister Grace, with a puffy helmet of blond hair and a hand-knit reindeer sweater. She kept her black patent leather purse strapped to her elbow at all times and was always the first to ask the uncomfortable question. Then she'd put on her kindly older lady expression and smile until she got an answer.

Adele looked Mike up and down. "My goodness. You're a strapping fellow."

"Mmm, thanks."

"A pilot, like Nicholas?"

"That's right."

She *tch*ed. "Too dangerous."

"Can be."

"Especially for a married man."

Behind Merry, Shannon muttered beneath her breath. Aunt Adele had been under everyone's skin at one time or another. With Shannon, it was calling her up every time there was a report of a downed jet or even a helicopter, "just to check" that Nicky hadn't been involved.

"I'm not a married man," replied Mike.

"I hear you had a fiancée," Adele said. "She jilted you."

"Adele, please," Grace said.

"What? Isn't that what you said—he got a Dear John letter?" Adele hiked up her purse. "You think about that, Meredith, before making any plans. And that's all I'm going to say."

"Promise?" Merry said behind her hand.

Adele had turned away. "Now, where's Charlie? I have to give that big lug a hug. Diane, you take my cheesy potatoes to the kitchen, please. I made a portion for Charlie without any cheese or salt. I'm certain they'll taste like foam, but orders are orders."

Shannon took Diane, who lived four states away and said that was just barely far enough, into the kitchen to drop off their potluck dishes, then on a tour of the home's absurdly ostentatious decorations—Charlie's pride and joy.

Merry gave Mike a poke. "Count your lucky stars. You got off light. But the day is long."

"Aw, she's not so bad."

"That's what everyone thinks, the first time the needle goes in. You wait until you're bristling like a porcupine and then see how sanguine you feel."

But she went away from the encounter with a weight lifted off her shoulders. Mike could handle himself. He certainly wasn't the kind who'd let a nosy aunt scare him off.

Unlike Greg, who'd come to Christmas once, been appalled by the folksiness and lack of amenities, and thereafter declared that whenever she felt the need for a hometown visit, he'd book himself into a golf resort on the opposite end of the country. Perhaps she should have taken that as a sign of their incompatibility, but at the time she'd mostly been relieved that she wouldn't have to deal with him trying to order soy cappuccinos at the town diner, where coffee came black, in one size, and cost forty-nine cents.

She went into the kitchen, threw together an asparagus salad, then whisked up a sweet dressing with extra virgin olive oil, a dollop of dijon mustard and a good squeeze of honey. Most of the guests would ignore the salad in favor of the macaroni salad or Jell-O molds, but she felt better having a healthy side dish on hand to fill out her father's plate.

Shannon entered. "Grace sent me in to see if you had the kitchen under control." She grinned. "Do you?"

Merry slung a towel over her shoulder. "Sure. Just open me a bottle of wine, will you?"

"No getting drunk this early."

"Not later, either, for me. And this is the one day I could really use a stiff drink."

"Oh, gosh." Shannon put an apron on over her nice dress before she began the task of peeling foil and arranging the buffet. "Remember the time we stole your uncle's flask?"

Merry chuckled as she removed a pan of hot rolls from the oven. "They overturned every cushion in the house, searching for it."

"Then claimed they were playing a game with the boys when your mother complained."

"And we thought the whiskey tasted horrible, but were so impressed with ourselves for daring to try it."

"What was I, only fifteen or sixteen?" Shannon calculated. "That might have been my very first York Christmas dinner. I was already dead gone on Nicky, but I didn't stop to think that meant your parents might someday become my in-laws."

"Would you have been more cautious?"

"Nah. Nicky had promised to kiss me under the mistletoe. That was the only thing on my mind, until you told me that a nip from the flask would put an extra flibbertigibbet in my tongue."

"It must have. Nicky's been obsessed with the mistletoe ever since."

Their laughter ended with a long, satisfying hug. When they pulled apart, Shannon's eyes were exceptionally bright. "I'm glad our children are going to have the chance to grow up together."

"Me, too." Merry made a face. "Even if that means putting up with Aunt Adele and her cheesy potatoes."

"And Grandpa Charlie's stories."

"And never having any privacy."

"There are always the closets," Shannon said with a chuckle.

"Closets." Merry hooted. "So that's why Nicky smells like mothballs!"

CHAPTER TEN

MORE RELATIVES ARRIVED. Then the pastor and his family, Jackie Marshak and company, and assorted singles, including Oliver Randall. Charlie held court from his easy chair, though whenever Grace was out of the room, he was back on his feet, adjusting the stove flue, sneaking a flask refill to one of the uncles, racing electric cars with the boys.

"It was only angina," he told Oliver, who couldn't get his car out of the corner. "But my Grace is a fuss-budget, so I'm letting her baby me. It makes her feel better."

Oliver concentrated on the toggle of the control box. Although the car revved and whined, it wouldn't budge.

"Give that over," Jackie said, taking the controls. She pressed the toggle. "You need to reverse, and then drive." The car took off like a shot, running over Aunt Adele's foot as it made a wide turn around the room.

She let out a startled yip. "Jackie Marshak, was that you? You're as bad your boys!"

"Just as fast, too," she said sassily and went to join the race down the hallway.

"That one's a pistol," Charlie said.

"I'd like to pull her trigger," muttered the uncle who'd had one too many nips from the flask.

Oliver turned as red as the cherry in his drink.

"Here ya go," said the uncle. He poured a dollop into Oliver's glass. "You look like you could use a nip or two or twenty."

"YOU DON'T MIND, do you, Mike?" Noelle plopped herself into his lap without waiting for permission. "There's nowhere left to sit. Besides…" She wriggled, leaning toward his ear. "This'll give both Merry and Aunt Adele something to think about."

Mike cranked his head back. "And what about Jeff?"

Noelle glanced at the erstwhile boyfriend, who was glaring at them from across the room. "Don't worry about him. He knows what a big ole flirt I am."

"Doesn't look like he's happy about it."

"I've got to keep him on his toes."

"Maybe he'd prefer to be treated nicely, for a change."

"Ooh, am I going to get a lecture?" Noelle flicked her hair. "How do you know I don't treat him nicely? In private, I'm real good at nice."

"You need to practice that in public, too."

"Scandalous!"

He laughed. "You know what I mean."

"I know that I'm only twenty and everyone in this family thinks I should march directly into the York-dom of happily married couples. Why can't they concentrate on getting Merry into line first? I'd say her case is more time-sensitive."

Noelle wound an arm around the back of his neck. She played with his hair, up top, where there was a little curl for her fingers to sink in. "Stop it," he said, batting her hand away. "You're only doing that to annoy Jeff."

She ignored the command and returned for another foray. "What about you and Merry? Is it serious?"

"I'm not playing around, I can tell you that."

"You'd better not be, 'cause I think she's falling for you in a hard way."

If Shannon or Nicky had made the comment, he'd have taken it dead serious. With Noelle, he couldn't be sure that she wasn't simply trying to get a rise out of him. Even so, he had to believe that Merry's feelings had become apparent and that *he* was the hold-out. When did being extremely careful about your commitments turn into a psychological stumbling block?

"Uh, well." He coughed. "I am due back on base in a couple of days. And there are other considerations."

Noelle's mouth stretched into a thin line. "Uh-huh."

"What does that mean?"

She shrugged. "I guess I thought you were more honest than that."

"YOU'RE STARTING to get big, Meredith."

"Not that big," Diane protested. "My tummy may be larger than hers and I've grown mine the natural way, via a six-pack of root beer and a bag of Doritos."

"That, my dear, is another issue," Adele said with a puckered glance at her daughter's well-padded figure. She returned to Merry. "How far along are you, now?"

"Pretty soon it'll be six months." Merry resisted the urge to touch the baby bump. After Noelle's comments about being a wimp, she'd deliberately avoided the loose sweaters and dresses that hid her shape and put on a nice silk blouse. It hung loose over a pair of navy slacks that zippered most of the way. A long gold chain necklace looped twice around, swinging about when she moved and framing her rounded middle. A small defiance, but something.

"No more hiding the pregnancy," Aunt Adele observed with a tinge of satisfaction.

Merry laughed lightly. "Gosh. Is there anyone left to hide from?"

"How about the father?"

Merry took a step back. "Don't worry yourself about him, Aunt Adele. He knows. We've worked things out."

Adele's head tilted. She took on her most kindly smile. "Did you ever tell us who the father is?"

Diane ripped off the plastic wrap and thrust a dessert plate at her mother. "Have a fudge bar," she insisted, which gave Merry an opening to flee.

"Not before dinner." Adele fluttered in a circle, dismayed that Merry had slipped from her grasp. She turned back to eye her daughter. "About your weight problem, my dear."

"LASAGNA'S GOOD," said uncle Frank to the Methodist pastor.

"Yup."

Nicky chewed, swallowed, wiped his mouth. "I like the spicy blue cheese chicken wings."

"What's that green stuff?"

"Vegetables. My wife made me take it."

"Potatoes are a vegetable."

"They're a starch."

"Who cares, as long as they're smothered in cheese."

The pastor departed.

Nicky craned his neck toward the buffet. "They put out the dessert?"

"Nope. I'm getting thirds."

MERRY CORNERED Jackie in the mud room, which bulged with coats, boots and assorted winter accessories. "What's happening with you and Oliver?"

"Not much. I invited him over after the Parade of Lights, y'know? To warm up, I said. He takes that literally. Spent a half hour sitting on one of my radiators. The one that doesn't even work." Jackie clenched her fingers in her hair. "How could a man that smart be so dense?"

"He's Oliver. You have to consider him a long-term project. Start off subtle, as friends, and work up to the romantic part."

"'Warming up,' wasn't subtle?"

Merry pulled a wry smile. "Apparently too subtle."

"The thing is, he barely talks. How can I get to know him?"

"You've read his books, that should give you a few clues."

"Yeah, sure, *Marianne's Homecoming*. I'm all clued in to his unrequited love affair with you."

Merry groaned. "I'll have a word with him. I don't know what I'll say, but it's past time he got over that ancient crush."

"Seriously?" Jackie blinked several times. "Because I kind of wondered if Ol was your backup plan, like if other things don't work out."

Merry cringed inwardly. "I don't have a plan. So I can't possibly have a backup plan."

"Hey, I saw how you came in and took over your mom and dad's business. Don't tell me you don't have a plan to give your baby a daddy."

"Ouch." Merry hesitated. "Why does everyone think my baby has to have a father?"

Jackie's brow furrowed, as if she didn't understand why Merry even needed to ask. "Because babies need fathers. That's just the way it is." She considered. "My exes weren't any prizes in the husband department, but at least they spend time with their sons. It's just too bad they're passing on their lunkheadedness. Having Oliver around would be a real good change of pace for Jimmy and Cory."

After a couple of attempts, Merry managed to force down the lump in her throat that had formed at the thought of her baby never having a daddy. All because she was too stubborn and independent to show a little flexibility and take a few chances.

"If that's what you want, make it happen."

"But how?" Jackie wailed.

Merry pointed up, then gave the dangling bunch of ragged greenery a second look. The stuff looked like it had been chewed on by mice. "When all else fails, get him under the mistletoe. Sometimes, one kiss is worth a thousand words."

"NAME FIVE WAYS chocolate is better than a man," Diane said to the small group of women of various ages.

"Hershey's, Lindt, Dove…" one of them began.

"No, really. Because I've got to give up one or the

other. Michael Kavanaugh and this chocolate revel bar are looking equally good."

"Let Merry have him. I'm taking these fudge bars to bed instead."

"You're naughty, Mary Alice."

"I'm realistic. Chocolate never cheated on me the way my ex did."

Diane sighed. "Most likely because it's on you. Forever."

"The diet begins January first. For now, a little extra indulgence won't hurt."

"Enablers," Diane said darkly as she bit into the gooey, nutty bar. She let out a moan of ecstasy.

"I HOPE YOU'RE enjoying yourself," Merry said to Oliver. "It can get kind of madcap around here on Christmas day."

"I noticed." He lifted a foot as an electric car buzzed past.

"Sorry about that." She would have to get even with Mike for giving the boys such annoying toys.

There was an awkward pause before Oliver blurted, "Thanks for the pen. That was thoughtful of you." The gift exchange had been going on through-out the day and early evening. Modest items were the norm, and though there was no formal drawing of names, it usually worked out that every guest received at least one gift.

"You're welcome. Oh, and guess what? I started one of your books. *Marianne's Homecoming.*"

"Uh, that's great." Oliver's eyes seemed ready to pop past his lenses.

"Is it… Does it…" Merry swallowed and tried again. "I apologize for being so blunt, but by any chance, are you still carrying a torch for me?"

He made a gurgling sound.

"You know that I've always liked you as friend, and honestly, I almost said yes when you asked me out that time. But that was years and years ago."

"It's fiction." The words burst from Oliver like bird shot. "I might have used real-life inspiration, but I'm not, uh, I'm not still hoping we will—that is, unless you're saying…"

Merry wasn't certain she'd followed his meaning, but it seemed like a good time to bring Jackie into the conversation. "Is there someone else you're interested in?"

Oliver shifted nervously.

"Because Jackie thinks you're wonderful. Did you know that she's read all of your books?"

"All of them? She never said."

"Every single one. She's dazzled. But perhaps a little intimidated. I know she doesn't come across that way, but it's true. She may be thinking you're too smart for her."

"But she's…" He blinked. "She's very bright. She knew all about solenoid poisoning."

"If you talk to her more, make her feel comfortable, I think that'll help."

His brow wrinkled. "Make her feel comfortable?"

And forget about yourself. "I think you'd love getting to know her and her sons." Merry briefly clasped his hands. "And they could use a man like you in their lives."

While Oliver didn't look convinced, at least her words seemed to set him thinking. He wandered off with his hands thrust deep in his pockets.

"WHAT ARE YOU DOING?" Shannon said with a muffled laugh. "Let me out. We're adults, not teenagers. We can't do this anymore."

"Would you rather I kissed you in front of mom, dad, Aunt Adele and God?"

"I see your point. But is the hall closet any better?"

"It has mistletoe."

"Excuse me?"

Nicky took her hand and guided it to the shelf ledge where he'd tacked up a sprig. "I put them up all over the house. Wait'll you see our bedroom."

"Nicholas! Aunt Adele will probably stick her head in there. You know how nosy she is."

"Eh, give the old girl a thrill. She'll go home wondering what kinky things you do to me with mistletoe."

Shannon giggled. "You'd better kiss me fast, then, before she notices we're gone."

Their mouths found each other unerringly. The kiss was long and luxurious, though it tasted slightly of blue cheese.

"Merry Christmas, honey. I love you so much."

"I love you, Nicky."

"Then can we please stay a little longer?"

"One more kiss," she agreed, moving even closer, although as far as she was concerned they never truly left each other's arms—or hearts.

JEFF MARTTI GROANED. "What are you doing to me?"

"I think you know." Noelle pounced atop him on the jouncy single bed. She gave him another kiss to keep him quiet, then sat astride his supine body, flicking bits of mistletoe across his silly fisherman's sweater. It was like he thought the price of admission to the York Christmas potluck was the dweebiest sweater a guy could wear. She much preferred Jeff in his usual soccer jersey or even the ratty football sweatshirt that was stained with pitch.

"Take off that stupid sweater," she demanded.

"No way." He wrestled her hands away. "I'm not getting into trouble with your parents. Again. You know what happened when your dad caught us out in the groves that time."

"They're two floors away, plus it's bedlam down there. They won't hear a thing."

Footsteps scurried by in the hall. "But someone else could."

Noelle threw herself off Jeff, rolling over with a pillow instead. She kissed it like an adolescent practicing her technique. "Mr. Pillow has no inhibitions."

"Maybe it's not inhibitions holding me back. You ever think of that, Noelle?" Jeff sat on the edge of the bed, not even chuckling at her bit with the pillow. "Maybe it's seeing you flirt with every man at the party. And at the parade. And the festival."

"So what? I'm a free spirit."

"Do you have to be free all the time?"

She stroked the pillow. *Way to kill the mood, Jeff.* "Nope. Just some of the time."

He sighed. "Yeah, that's what I figured."

"Look, I'm sorry," Oliver said when Jackie tried to kiss him beneath the mistletoe in the entry room. Since he was a foot taller, she'd had to launch herself like a gymnast mounting an apparatus. The attempt had been awkward at best. "I don't have much experience with this kind of thing."

"What about Dolly at the Kiwanis picnic? She told everyone she did you in the back of her van."

He clutched the stocking cap he'd pulled down over his ears in preparation of his departure. "What?"

"Dolly said she did you—"

"I heard what you said."

Oliver had gone so pale Jackie thought he might faint. She put her arms around his waist. Strictly for reassurance and support, not because she was trying to make another pass. On the other hand, if he keeled over on top of her, that'd be the most action she'd had in years.

Holding out for your hero sucked sour eggs.

Oliver looked like an ostrich when he gulped. Jackie thought that was just adorable. She was such a goner.

"Listen," he said. "Dolly did something in the back of that van, but it wasn't me."

"Does that mean you're a…"

"No!"

"Oh, well, that would be okay if you were, as long as you didn't expect me to be one, too."

"I had a life before I moved to Christmas, you know."

"Probably a much more exciting one." She cocked her head, trying to see past his glasses. "Maybe you could tell me about it sometime."

"Maybe." His head jerked back. "What are you doing?"

"Taking off your glasses."

"Why?"

"We're still standing under the mistletoe."

He blinked and let her remove the heavy spectacles. He said, "You want to try again?" as if he couldn't believe he hadn't already blown his last chance. The tops of his ears and the tip of his nose were bright pink.

"Just tell me one thing," Jackie said. "Would you rather be standing here with Merry?"

Oliver took a couple of seconds to answer, and she appreciated that. He was a thinker. He didn't take things lightly. She knew she could count on his answer being as honest as he could make it.

He stared directly into her eyes, his gaze as penetrating as the most commanding of heroes, and even though she knew that he was probably only trying to see her, she was thrilled to the quick.

"I'm certain, Jackie," he said. "I want to kiss only you."

This time, she let him stoop to her level. When he did, his lips puckered as if he expected to plant one on a fish. She couldn't resist wrapping her arms around his neck to hold him there, especially after she felt his lips relax into a comfortable fit.

Jackie closed her eyes. He might be kissing only her, but he sure better not be planning only one kiss.

"PARTY'S WINDING DOWN," Mike said from his seat midway up the staircase to the second floor.

Merry had just emerged from checking on her dad, whom Grace had insisted on putting to bed early even though he said there was plenty of party remaining in both him and the evening.

She edged sideways around Mike, but then sat, one step down, and rested her arm and head on his thigh as easily as longtime friends…or lovers. "I'm beat. I can't remember the potluck being this exhausting before."

"You did a lot of work." Every time he'd tried to get near, she'd hurried off to the kitchen or the dining room on a frantic food emergency.

"Now I know how Mom cooks so much fattening food but still keeps fit. She keeps too busy to eat."

Mike stroked her hair. "You might also be tired because you're—"

"Hey. Not that word."

"Not even between us?"

"Mmm, maybe us." She drew back, sending a sweet-faced glance at him. "The baby's been active today. I've felt her moving quite a lot, but I didn't want to draw attention by telling anyone."

He bumped down a step so they were side by side. He looked at her round belly, but he didn't put a hand out to feel, even though he wanted to. "How'd that go—did you field a lot of inquiries?"

She chuckled. "What a way to put it." Then shrugged. "I must admit it wasn't bad at all. Aunt Adele got in a few jabs, but then she'll always find something to comment on. Maybe I have been too self-conscious. A wimp, like Noelle said."

"I don't know. I sort of like that you're not the brazen type. These days, a little modesty is a rare thing."

"You always say the right thing." Merry sighed and

was about to lean against him again when she sat up straighter instead. "Oops. There she goes!"

"The baby? How does it feel?"

"Like a goldfish. There's just a tiny flutter every now and then." She put her hand to her middle. "I don't know if you can feel the movement from the outside yet."

He could tell that she wanted him to try. But he couldn't. Touching her in such an intimate way would be too much. It would be real. Thus far, he could still put his week in Christmas down to a vacation that was more than he'd expected, but not so huge that he'd never…never…

Never forget.

Too late for that. He might be able to move on, but he wasn't likely to forget.

"You called the baby 'she'," he said.

"I don't know the sex. But I usually think of it as a girl. I'd be just as thrilled with a boy, naturally, but it's a little easier to imagine myself with a girl."

"Why?"

Her brows pulled together. "To be honest, it's because I'm afraid a boy will be a constant reminder of, uh, you know."

"The biological father."

"That's probably a silly worry. Friends with children say that babies get their own personalities pretty quickly. If I have a boy, he'll be his own unique person just as much a girl."

"You don't ever mention that you might meet someone in the future and get married."

"That could happen, sure. I suppose it probably will. I'm just not counting on it." She stole a glance. "I do not want to be one of those women who is desperate to latch on to a man. Any man." She put her chin on her hands. "And that's why it bugs me when my mother and her pals are always hinting about who'd make a good father."

"You want to fall in love first."

"Mmm-hmm. Given my condition, it's a delicate negotiation."

There was a moment's silence, and she must have realized what she'd said because she suddenly snapped out of the dreamy mood. After throwing a wary look at him, she started to hoist herself off the steps.

"Hey, hey, wait," he said, catching her hand. "Don't run. I'm not."

"I don't know why you aren't." She dropped back down with an embarrassed groan. "I didn't mean that I was falling in love right now. I know it may have sounded that way, but that's not what I was saying. Even if it was, I would never put that kind of pressure on a man I met only a few days ago, so please don't—"

He kissed her.

Her mouth was open and soft and warm with the breath she gulped back when he caught her by surprise. He felt a flutter—many of them. Her lashes, her racing pulse, the nerves in his own hollow stomach. Regardless of the massive potluck buffet, he was always empty and yearning, especially when she was around.

"If I need an excuse," he said with his eyes closed, "there's a pinch of mistletoe in my pocket."

She laughed softly, with her forehead resting against his nose. "Mine, too."

"Nicky?"

"He stuck them up all over the house."

"Smart man."

With a sigh of pleasure, they came together again, grateful for a reason not to talk, only to feel.

UNCLE FRANK STOOD ALONE, overly stuffed and pleasantly squiffed. He looked about blearily, supposing that he might have overlooked the departure of a few of the guests. Still, the house seemed to be half as full as it'd been ten minutes ago. Even Adele was looking for a target.

"Whazza," he said, stupidly drawing her bead. "Where did everyone go, eh?"

CHAPTER ELEVEN

MERRY BREATHED DEEPLY. "The cold air feels good, doesn't it?"

"Only a Northerner would say that," Mike teased, although she could tell that he knew what she meant. He breathed like a cartoon bull, with plumes of vapor coming out both nostrils. Any second, she expected him to snort and paw the porch.

"Humph." He frowned at her. "Get back inside before you catch a chill, woman."

"Give me a minute." She'd grabbed an old sweater from a hook to step outside and wave away the last of the guests. Red brake lights blinked out among the trees. "The house is too warm. I was feeling claustrophobic."

"Come here, then." He didn't wait for her, just enveloped her with his body and kissed the top of her head. She had to admit that he felt even better than the lungful of fresh air. And not claustrophobic at all.

Their hug was hard but brief. They broke apart and went back inside. Grace was just disappearing up the stairs.

"We made a deal," Nicky explained. "She's turning in for the night and we're cleaning up after the party."

"You're cleaning up," Shannon said, coming through the hallway with her children. Kathlyn was asleep on her shoulder. "I'm putting these ones to bed."

Skip scowled. "It's too early, Mom."

"You can read or watch TV for a while, but you're going up. You must be tired. You've been running around all day."

"Can I get my Bionicles to work on?"

"Quickly." Shannon whispered to Merry. "I'll be back down as soon as the kids are settled."

"No, you're pooped. Let me finish up with the guys. The food's put away, there's just the dishwasher to load and some picking up to be done."

"Grace will be listening for the vacuum cleaner," Shannon warned as she went upstairs.

"Boots at the controls," Nicky said cheerfully, wheeling the device from the hall closet.

Merry let out a groan when she walked through the disaster area of the dining room and family room, where most of the action had taken place.

Mike appeared a minute later with an empty garbage bag. He began shoveling off the surfaces cluttered with plastic cups and plates, wads of gift wrap and discarded packaging. "Sanitation service," he announced. "At your request."

She waved an arm. "Clean sweep it, sir!"

Their male vigor energized her. She rinsed and loaded dishes, stepped around the vacuum Nicky wielded and scrubbed down the countertops and tables. While the men took out the trash and brought in a few armfuls of wood, she sorted out the Christmas music and plumped pillows before finally allowing herself to sink down onto the couch.

Another Christmas accomplished.

She patted her belly. "Next year," she whispered. "Merry Christmas, baby."

There was a clatter from the mud room as the wood box was filled, then the sound of stomping feet and more of the snorting bull sounds.

Merry realized who was missing. "Where's Noelle?" she asked as the men returned to the family room.

"She took off a half hour ago." Nicky shrugged. "Plans with Jeff."

"I thought they'd argued."

"It wouldn't be Christmas without a drama from Noelle." Nicky perched on the arm of their father's chair and let out a huge yawn. He scrubbed his face with both hands. "Are we done? I'm ready to collapse."

"We're done."

He came over and kissed her cheek. "Merry Christmas, Mer."

She squeezed his hand. "Merry Christmas, Nicky."

Her brother flicked his chin at Mike in male short-hand. "You've got the fire?"

"Yep." At the woodstove, Mike had stirred up the coals. He put down the poker, but he didn't close the door, nor even look up. He seemed deep in thought, with one hand thrust into the pocket of his pants. His fist bunched.

"'Night, then." Nicky departed. "Leave a light on the porch for Noelle."

Merry shifted, stretched. "I'm heading up soon."

"Right." Mike pulled something from his pocket, gave it a brief glance, then crumpled it into a ball and tossed it on top of the bed of coals. A small blaze flared. After watching the flame for a minute, he closed the heavy door and dropped the latch with a clang. "That's that."

Merry's scalp tingled. "What?"

He looked at her as if he'd forgotten that she—or anyone—was in the room. His face displayed a moment of inner hesitation before clearing. "It was only a letter," he said. "A Dear John letter."

"Oh, I see." *The* Dear John letter, she said to herself, not supposing there was more than one.

She toed off her shoes and pulled one leg up on the couch, catching it around the knee. She needed to hold on to something, because there was a rushing river inside her, the kind that flooded the banks and swept up everything in its path.

Carefully, she cleared her throat. "Should I be startled you kept it all this time, or pleased that you've burned it up?"

Mike's brow creased. "I don't really know."

She patted the couch. "Come sit with me for a minute. Tell me a story."

He hung the poker on the rack, then went and shut off lamps until the room's only sources of illumination were the colored lights of the Christmas tree and the red glow of the banked fire through the glass on the woodstove door. With a creak of cold timbers, the farmhouse settled into the darkness and quiet of a winter night.

"I didn't keep the letter for emotional reasons," Mike said as he sat beside her. "At least not the ones you'd assume."

"I'm assuming nothing." Except that alarms were going off inside. He'd seemed so even-keeled about the whole broken-engagement thing. She hadn't felt more than a moment's worry about whether or not he was still attached.

It seemed she'd been wrong. Maybe.

"I'm not hung up on Denise, if that's what you're thinking."

"Well, that's good." Merry swallowed.

The question hung between them. Why hold on to the letter?

"I didn't know why I kept the letter for so long,"

he said. "Except lately, I think maybe I've started to figure it out." He lifted his chin and sniffed at the wood smoke that hung in the air.

She watched his gaze travel along the ceiling. "What are you looking for?"

"Smoke detectors."

"There." She pointed to an alarm attached above the doorway, where a small green light blipped every minute or so. "We have them all over the house."

"Have the batteries been checked? Do they also detect carbon monoxide? That's a concern, when you're burning wood or gas."

"I'm certain they do." She remembered his father's accidental death and added, "Don't worry," in a soothing tone. "See the green light? That shows the alarm's working. Not that there's much chance of it ever being silent. My dad seems to set off the alarm at least once a week when he fusses with the stove."

She stroked her palm across Mike's shoulders. "We're safe."

He rolled his neck. "Of course."

"What do the alarms have to do with the letter?"

His head hung forward. When he finally answered, his voice was scraped as raw as an old dirt road. "Like I said, I didn't know why I kept it. I just couldn't let go. Not of Denise, but the…commitment, I suppose. And the feeling that I'd failed." He kept his elbows on his widespread knees, but his head swiveled to look at her. His eyes were imploring. "I see now that it's about how I lost my dad when I was young. The guilt of that."

"But you—"

"I know. It was an accident. Not my fault." He shook his head. "That doesn't matter. In my heart, I vowed a long time ago that I never wanted to be responsible for anyone but myself. I broke that when I asked Denise to marry me, but the thing is, in retrospect, I knew the feelings between us weren't strong enough to last. You see what I mean? The commitment wasn't real."

Merry looked away. Her chest ached. She could guess what he would say next. It should have made her feel happy, and instead...

His hand reached for hers across the cushions. The grip of his fingers was like a vise, squeezing her heart until it hurt. "But it's real with you, Merry."

"The feelings," she said.

He nodded.

She nodded, too, and tightened her hold on his hand. Her life was flowing by without her. She was stranded on a tiny island with Mike and he was about to jump off. She could feel him slipping away. "I know what you're saying."

His voice became the barest croak. She could hear the strain as he held on by his fingertips. "I don't think so."

"No, I do. You're telling me that because this is serious, we can't continue." She pulled free and wrapped her hands into a knot under her chin. "It's not a surprise. I've known all along. I wasn't expecting anything else, Mike, so please don't beat yourself up just because other people might have had different hopes."

The stairs creaked. Merry didn't stir, keeping her hands tucked beneath her chin and her burning lids lowered even when her mother appeared in the doorway, wrapped in a thick terry cloth robe. "I'm making a cup of tea before bed. Would either of you like some?"

"No, thanks, Mrs. York."

Silently, Merry shook her head.

Her mother hovered questioningly, but for once she didn't ask what was going on. "I'll only be a minute, then."

"We're on our way up," Mike said. "I'll take your tray."

"Thank you, Michael." She padded into the kitchen.

After a minute, he said, "Merry?"

"I'm fine." She sighed. "It's been a long day."

"Give me your hand. Just for a minute."

She let him take it. "Don't say anything else, okay? Let's just sit."

Her eyes closed. She concentrated on his hand linked with hers. The sense of movement inside her had slowly regained its strength after the interruption, but now she knew that it was going nowhere. There was tonight, tomorrow. There was no more beginning, only the end. And she had to be okay with that, just the way she'd been telling herself that she was, all along.

The kettle whistled. They both flinched.

"Okay," Merry said. "I'll get the tree lights."

It could be a sad thing, shutting off the Christmas tree when Christmas was over. She yanked the cord fast. The room plunged into darkness. She turned away before the afterimage of the bright tree faded from her eyes.

Mike emerged from the kitchen with the tea tray. Grace followed. "Noelle's not home yet?"

"It's early yet, Mom. I'll wait up for her." Merry didn't look at Mike. "I'm taking a bath before bed anyway."

They climbed the stairs. Merry said a quick good-night and proceeded to the next floor. She didn't want to wait for Mike, nor see the subdued and regretful longing in his eyes.

Submerged in hot water that cooled too quickly in the drafty third-floor bathroom, she stayed in the tub for a good half hour. She kept hoping her physical desire would leak away, that she would no longer be tempted by the notion of creeping into the guest bedroom in the middle of the night.

Of course, she'd never actually do that.

Not above her mother's nose.

She dried off, wrapped her hair in a towel turban, listened by the door to be certain the way was clear, then darted across the hallway to her temporary bedroom.

She heard Mike moving around next door. He went into the bathroom and she pulled her knees to her chest, holding herself in as if otherwise she'd fly apart into pieces from her spot in the center of the narrow single bed. Only after he'd returned to his room did she move again, grabbing a hair dryer from Noelle's unzipped luggage. The house was too cold to go to bed with wet hair.

The dryer was loud and she relaxed, running the hot air through her hair. She didn't bother with a comb, only used her tunneling fingers. The warmth and noise made her feel almost normal.

The silence came back with a vengeance as soon as she'd unplugged the dryer. Aware of every sound she made, she got Oliver's book and climbed under the covers to read.

For an hour, she tried to concentrate and managed only a few pages. At least the book wasn't familiar. In her current state, she'd have curled up and died if her inner thoughts had been revealed on the page. But the woman in the book wasn't her, no more than the hero was Mike. Make that Oliver.

She didn't know who or what she was. She didn't know anything.

With the book tucked away and the reading lamp shut off, she stretched out, waiting for Noelle's headlights to shine through the thin cotton of the curtains.

Everyone else would be asleep by now.

Maybe not Mike.

She sat up, peeled off her robe, then burrowed back under the covers. She tried her right side, her left side, then lying flat on her back and twiddling her toes.

She counted her breaths. Her heartbeat.

What was she doing?

Just fall asleep. He doesn't want you.

No, he wanted her. He just wouldn't promise to keep her. Which was a funny sticking point, when she thought about it, seeing that she hadn't asked him to.

Oh, hell. Thinking in that direction would lead her down the wrong path.

Her legs twitched. Wanting to go there.

"No." She rolled onto her side and closed her eyes.

Either she fell asleep, or the few moments rest got her mind to finally stop spinning. When she blinked her eyes open again, the frantic, scrambling thoughts were gone. She was warm and peaceful, the quiet inside her matching the silence of the house. Moonlight shone through the eyelet curtains, illuminating the snowflakes that fell against the glass in snow-globe spirals.

The ironic snow globe. She'd forgotten to give it to Mike.

With no more angst to stop her, it made perfect sense that she should get out of bed, find the gift and step on stocking-clad feet to the guest room next door. She didn't knock. That would be too loud.

The knob turned soundlessly. The room was dark, but she could make out that Mike was asleep. No reason not to leave the gift on the bureau where he'd find it in the morning.

He said, "Merry?" before she'd managed three steps into the room.

She froze. "Shhh."

His head moved on the pillow. "What are you doing?" he whispered.

"Dropping off a gift. I forgot to put it under the tree."

"What is it?"

"Shhh." She inched over to the bed and bent down so her voice was not even a whisper. More like the barest intimation of sound. "It's nothing, really. A memento."

He took the small present from her and undid the twist of red tissue paper. He held a small jar filled with fluid. "I don't get it."

"It's a snow globe." Shivers prickled at her bare legs and she climbed onto the bed on her knees without thinking, or at least without thinking much. "I bought it for a buck at the kids' art exhibit." She took the tiny item from him and held it up to the light coming in the window. "See? It's handmade from a baby-food jar."

"A baby-food jar?"

Ah, then he did see the irony. She placed it on his palm, bottom up.

He rose onto an elbow. His chest was bare. "Merry? What are you doing here?"

"Shhh." She traced the rickrack clumsily glued to the base of the snow globe, then folded his fingers around it. She covered his loose fist with both of her hands and gave them a shake.

"There's glitter inside," she said, when she'd pried his fingers open and revealed the tiny jar swirling with white and silver specks. Glued to the inside of the cap was a small pine cone.

"Okay. Thanks."

"Shhh," she said, leaning forward to kiss him. "Can I crawl under the covers with you? The room is cold."

He moved his lips away. "That's probably not a good idea."

She slithered over him, not much concerned with modesty. Her T-shirt slid higher up her thighs as she bent her legs, reaching them past the upper edge of the blankets. "Don't worry," she said to Mike's back. "I just want to get warm. I won't make you sign any papers."

"God, Merry."

"Teasing." She moaned. The warmth in the bed was bliss. "I've been thinking, and I want to make this a most memorable Christmas for both of us." She pressed against him, draped her right arm over his body and touched her palm to the center of his chest. His skin was smooth and warm, finely textured, even the patch of chest hair. She didn't let that distract her.

She wanted to feel his heart. It wouldn't say no.

He was still resisting. "This isn't the way."

"I think it is. Let me give us both a gift. A real one, not a joke like the snow globe."

"It won't be that easy." He turned his head and she saw the furrow of his brow. "For one thing—"

"I know. You think that no matter what I say, I'll still take the sex as some kind of commitment. Well, I'm a mature woman. I know that consenting adults can have a good time without it being the start of something serious. Especially when one of them is leaving to travel hundreds, or maybe even thousands of miles away."

She stroked his chest. She kissed the back of his shoulder. She whispered against his nape. "Let me give you this. Let me have this. Just as a memory. That's all I want. A memory."

He shuddered.

"Only a memory," she breathed. "Not a promise."

"Merry," he said gruffly, turning over onto his back. He took her hand, squeezed it, seemed about to speak. She could feel his honor and righteousness gathering force, and she closed her eyes to withstand the rejection—but he didn't say a word.

He made a sound.

"Shhh."

Engulfed with relief, she laughed shakily under her breath. "Noelle's not home yet. Everyone else is asleep. They won't hear us."

"Still, we have to be careful."

She kissed his knuckles, loosening his grip enough so that she could walk her fingers along the firm swell of his pectoral muscles. "Careful, and silent as mice."

Her other hand played across his ribs, where the rising of each breath told her how hard he'd fought for control before giving in. He exhaled and would have rolled onto his side to reach for her, but she moved first, following her exploring hands with her body, fitting herself against him, with one thigh nudging between his legs, her breasts and belly filling his hollows, her head tucking into the nook of his neck. She murmured there, burbling with the sweet nothings of the pleasure she'd craved for so long.

"Nice." He held her hips. Warmth radiated from his palms, spreading through her from the inside out.

She sighed. "I could stay like this forever."

His chest vibrated beneath her. "I could, but I couldn't."

"Ah, men." His arousal was prominent, a solid bar of heat pressing near her thigh. She pushed a little closer, but kept her hand away. For now.

They had time. Time to be slow, and quiet, and easy. Time to revel in every sensation.

The only time they didn't have was more.

Threatened by the dash of uncertainty, she found Mike's mouth and let his kisses drive away any doubt that she wasn't doing the right thing. She wouldn't regret making love, that she knew with a blinding assurance. This one time would keep her warm for the remainder of the winter.

Their kisses became hotter, bolder. His hands moved past her hips, spanning her sides for a couple of minutes before reaching even higher.

Her T-shirt rode up between them. Normally, she would have stripped it off, but being pregnant made everything different. She wasn't ready to reveal herself that way. He must have sensed that, because he didn't rush, but slowed to stroke and caress all parts of her, even her belly, before finally reaching her breasts.

She released a moan. His hands were gentle but firm, touching her full, tender breasts exactly the right way. At last, the wrinkled tee seemed only a hindrance. They removed it together.

He sank lower, rocking the mattress with a creaking sound. "Shhh," she said, though she was laughing softly as she caught the edge of the blankets and pulled them past his head, up around her face as his mouth moved across her breasts and her shoulders curved inward to hold him even closer. His tongue flickered, lapped, suckled. Streaks of pleasure shot across her nerve endings.

She shivered when he left her, but it was only for a couple of seconds, to rummage through a leather kit at the bureau. He came back, bringing the delicious heat with him. Her desire had never left.

He turned her over onto her back and pulled off her panties, taking a moment to appreciate her, holding her baby bump between his hands, kissing the roundest part of her, before dragging the bedclothes up again.

They hugged, full body, until the luxury of feeling her skin against his skin became urgent with deeper need. She explored the wide expanse of his shoulders as he pushed down his pajama bottoms, made quick work of the condom and rose above her. She felt the ripple and flex of every muscle, the tension in his pent-up desire. Her legs opened and she pressed the flat of her hands into the base of his spine, experiencing their joining through his movement as he slowly entered her.

She let out only one small sound, a whimper of encouragement, before burying her face against his chest.

"Shhh," he said, nudging her chin up, then smiling at her as her head tilted back against the pillow.

She nodded, touching his face with her fingertips over and over, as if she couldn't see him in the dark and needed to reassure herself. But she could. She could see him and feel him and, yes, love him, too.

That was what she hadn't told him. She loved him.

Her memory wouldn't be about sex; it would be about love.

They rocked gently together in ebb and flow, sometimes kissing, sometimes caressing. He never quite let the tide turn into onrushing passion, keeping the stronger impulses under wraps. At least until the end, when her soft, warm body began to tighten and he drove deeper and faster, the bedsprings creaking as their pleasure crested. They clutched at each other, breaking the urge to call out into short, sharp gasps as they shuddered with their release.

Afterward, Merry couldn't move. She was a pool of melted butter. Fortunately, Mike wasn't going anywhere, either. She let herself slide into sleep, certain that there'd be plenty to say when morning came.

She would reassure him if she had to, again and again.

All the while keeping the best gift to herself.

His love, even if he never acknowledged giving it.

THE NIGHT WAS STILL and black when Mike awoke. He hadn't slept for long. Not even long enough to be surprised by the feel of Merry's round body snuggled beside him. Every detail of their encounter remained engraved in his mind.

Making a memory, she'd called it. No promises attached.

He didn't doubt her sincerity. But he knew it wasn't that simple. Almost nothing in life was.

That he'd gone along anyway showed him how weak he really was, when it came to Merry. Merry and child. Baby Merry, the impending bundle of joy and responsibility, both of the never-ending type.

Oh, man. Mike rammed his head back on the pillow, one hand pressed to his eyes. He'd gone and done it now. All his caution had served for nothing.

Eventually, a small, pitiful sound penetrated his roiling brain. Crying, he realized. If Merry hadn't been right there beside him, he'd have sworn it was her.

He nudged her awake. "Merry."

"Mmph. It can't be morning."

He held his hand loosely across her mouth. "Hush. Listen."

The sobs had abated, but after several seconds there came one more, followed by the jounce of bed-springs and a muffled whimper.

She tensed. "Who is it?" she whispered.

"Noelle, I'm guessing."

Merry sat up, pushed back her tousled hair. "Something must have gone wrong between her and Jeff." She crossed her arms over her bare breasts. "I'd better go."

He swept aside the blanket to find her T-shirt. The snow globe dropped to the rag rug with a small thud. He retrieved it, grateful to see that it hadn't cracked.

He shook the jar, making the glitter whirl, amused by Merry's cockeyed sense of the absurd.

Christmas. In a baby-food jar.

She kissed the top of his head. "See you tomorrow."

He clutched her wrist. "Wait." Suddenly, there was so much to say.

She extricated herself, bundled into her robe, looking no different at all than she had an hour or two ago, except that the trouble in her eyes had burnished to the glow of satisfaction.

"Tomorrow," she repeated, and tiptoed out.

CHAPTER TWELVE

MERRY LEANED AGAINST the door for a little while, re-
covering her bearings. There were a few times in life
when something so huge happened to a person that
it was hard to believe that the world around you didn't
reflect the change. Having a doctor confirm she was
expecting had been once such event. Making love
with Mike was another. If she'd looked out the
window and seen that the house had lifted off its
foundation and taken flight among the stars, she
wouldn't have been surprised.

Noelle snuffled into her pillow, pulling Merry's
head down from the clouds. Her sister was prone,
half-undressed, sprawled among a tangle of bedclothes. One bedside lamp burned.

"No-no," Merry whispered. She crossed the room
and eased down onto the edge of her sister's bed.
"What's wrong, honey?"

"Jeff." With a grunt, Noelle pulled the pillow over
her head. "He's going to ditch me."

"I can't believe that." Jeff had been Noelle's most

devoted admirer from kindergarten onward, give or take a few awkward teenage years. They went together like chips and salsa.

Noelle flipped. Her eyes were bloodshot. "He's tired of waiting for me. Is that fair? I can't help it that we met when I was still learning to tie my shoes." She jammed the back of her wrist against her nose. "Jeff used to do them for me. The knots made me mad."

Merry smiled. That sounded like her sister, all right. "What exactly did he say? Was it an ultimatum?"

"Just about. He didn't ask me to quit college or anything, but he wants me to…" She took a big breath and said, "Commit," as if it was a dirty word.

"What kind of commitment?"

"Just, you know, 'til death do us part."

"Marriage?" Merry's voice spiked higher than she'd meant it to.

Anyone could see that Noelle wasn't ready for marriage. But there was also a tiny part of Merry that flared up with envy for how easily her sister could have what seemed unlikely for herself. Because even though Noelle wasn't ready, Jeff was the right man. He'd always loved her with a pure and steady devotion.

"He didn't propose." Noelle threw her arms overhead. She'd put on a pajama top over panties and knee socks. "But he wants me to get serious. No more dating or flirting or even looking. Cripes, that really stinks."

"That's what you were crying over?"

"You're *old,* Mer. You don't understand."

"I'm thirty-six. Not that old."

"If I was thirty-six, I'd grab Jeff in one second flat. But now? It's too soon and even if I'm the only one, I'm darn sure that I'm being sensible to see that."

"You have a point." Merry swallowed. Thirty-six was not old. Thirty-six and pregnant, however… well, that was certainly rather doughty. From the outside. Inside, she was as scared as your average teenage single mom.

"Well, I wish Jeff could see that. He says I'm just being frivolous. So he's going to dump me." Noelle's lower lip trembled. "That's what I was crying about."

"Did you try to explain?"

"Um, sort of."

"Uh-oh. What did you do?"

Smiling rather grimly at the ceiling, Noelle pushed her tousled hair to the top of her head. "I vamped him. You know men can't think with both heads at once. Except this time it didn't work. He went right back to insisting I make a decision."

"Then maybe you should."

"Ugh. Easy for you to say." Noelle's hair tumbled free as she jackknifed up to a sitting position. She considered Merry with a squinted eye. "Wait a minute. Where'd you come from?"

"The bathroom."

"Nope. I was in there. You weren't, and you weren't in bed, and not downstairs, which means—oh, my God."

Merry held a finger to her lips. "Not so loud."

Noelle repeated, "Oh, my God," without making a sound. "On Christmas night?" she squeaked. "You naughty girl."

"Don't make this tawdry, Noelle."

Noelle sobered. "Right. You're serious about him."

"As serious as I can be, considering he's leaving. Tomorrow." For a week, she'd believed that tomorrow wouldn't come. Now it was after midnight, no longer Christmas, and Mike had only one more full day before he had to leave.

"That sucks."

Merry pulled the collar of her robe up around her face. "Yeah, it does."

Noelle turned her head onto its side. Her eyes narrowed as she leaned back on her arms. "What does Mike say?"

"What *can* he say?"

"Huh. Lots. Like that he's fallen for you at first sight and he thinks you're a fertile goddess and he can't possibly be expected to live without you."

Merry winced. "He's not ready."

"Great." Noelle frowned. "You've got a guy who can't commit, and I've got one who insists on it. Want to trade?"

"I want to go to bed." Merry was too tired for her sister's sass. And too tired to think, especially about Mike and how little time they had remaining.

They separated and climbed into their side-by-side beds. Noelle clicked off the light and settled down with a long sigh. After five minutes, a dry chuckle came from her side of the room. "Romance, schmomance," she said. "Marriage, schmarriage."

"Love," Merry said, thinking to join in. But she couldn't continue.

"Schmove," Noelle finished, without much enthusiasm.

Merry thought longingly of Michael's bed. She'd been very, very wrong.

One memory was not enough to sustain her.

AT LOOSE ENDS, Merry went into work the next morning. Jackie would return in a few days and they'd give the café and gift shop a thorough cleaning and inventory before shutting down for the remainder of the winter. In the meantime, she wanted to get more of the paperwork transferred to the computer, so she could work at home on her laptop and have all the numbers shipshape in time for the year's tax returns. Through April, she'd be bookkeeping, collating and gestating.

How exciting.

Her father dropped by midmorning. "I'll try not to get in your way," Charlie said, coming into the tiny office and doing just that, with a corner of his parka knocking over a cup of pens—she caught them—and his choppers brushing a stack of papers off the other corner of the desk when he turned to sit. He slapped the thick leather gloves against his palm. "I had to get out of the house. Your mother is driving me up the wall."

"You know you're welcome here anytime, Dad." Merry shoved the pens into the holder and set it in the middle of the desk. "I'm sorry if I've ever given you the opposite impression. I know that this is still your business."

"It's a family business," he said.

"But you'd run it for forty years, until I swooped in and took over. There are days I wonder if you regret retiring."

"Sometimes," he agreed with a grunt. "I didn't think it would be so hard, stepping back and letting you run the place on your own without getting to put in my two bits."

She smiled wryly. "Especially when I've been doing things so differently."

Charlie's eyes creased. "The outcome's the same. Maybe even better, eh?"

"I haven't run all the numbers yet, but we had a fairly good year, even with the popularity of faux trees."

Her father nodded. "So you should continue as you are, Mer. I'll adjust. I could take up golf."

"Golf would be good for you, Dad. But that doesn't mean you have to give up the business completely." She hesitated, reaching deep into the well of compromise, where she admittedly rarely went. It was hard to let go of her bossiness and independence, but she'd resolved to try, that day in the hospital. "We could always run the place together."

He chuckled. "You think that'd work?"

"We could try."

"No, that'd be asking for trouble. We'd be butting heads so often, one of us would wind up with a cracked skull." Charlie shifted around and slapped the choppers against his knee. "I'll just try to stay out of your way, kiddo."

He'd said *that* before, but retirement was too dull for him and he hadn't been able to keep away from the tree farm for more than a couple of days at a time.

She went back to the well. "What if I made you the tree lot manager?"

"That's Jeff's job."

"The *senior* tree lot manager. You could share all your knowledge with Jeff, prepare him to take over the job full-time in a few years. That end of the business isn't my strength anyway."

"Full-time?" Charlie fingered his white beard. "You think you can swing the salary?"

"If business continues to improve. And, um, you'd be providing your wisdom pro bono, of course." Her parents' retirement income was already in place.

Charlie's eyes twinkled. "It's a good plan, Meredith. Except for one thing."

She arched her brows.

"Are *you* going to be happy, living and working in Christmas?"

"I've already made that decision, Dad."

She looked down at her hands, folded atop the paperwork. Breakfast had been more awkward than chaotic. Nicky and Shannon were all wrapped up in each other as their time together grew short. Noelle had acted like a cranky lump, while Grace had watched every bite that Charlie had eaten. Mike had said nothing to her at all, only stolen a few wordless glances across the table.

Afterward, the men had proclaimed it was their day to take care of all the small, nagging household chores and errands that needed doing. Putting up a few window insulation kits, changing hard-to-reach lightbulbs, that kind of thing. Merry had fled to the office.

"Then nothing's changed?" her father prodded, and she knew that he was asking about her relationship with Mike, as discreetly as possible.

She took a deep breath and met his eyes even though her cheeks flared with heat. "No, Dad. Nothing's changed. I'm committed to running the York Tree Farm and raising my baby in Christmas—and that's it."

"Shannon and Nicky are going to dinner out of town," Mike said on the other end of the phone, later that day, after Merry had gone home from the office with a stack of files and plans to work so steadily she'd have no time to think about this being Mike's last night.

"Sounds romantic," she said.

"I thought we could do the same."

Schmomantic.

"I'm not up for the long drive." The worst thing about living in Christmas was not that there was no *there* there, it was having to travel for an hour to merely get within sight of a *there.*

"What about the Christmas Cheer? At least let me take you there."

Loud music, raucous customers, greasy food?

Perfect. They wouldn't be able to hear each other talk. Hence, she could avoid embarrassing revelations.

"That sounds okay," she said.

"Then it's a date."

Oh, no. Not a date. More like a…a *schmate.*

A non-schmomantic one.

"Pick you up in half an hour." Mike sounded relieved.

"An hour," she bargained. In an hour, the volume of the Cheer's crowd should have escalated just high enough to prevent much communication between them.

She hung up, immediately set aside her laptop and stripped off the oversize plaid shirt she'd just put on over a turtleneck. Girlish impulses, of the type she'd thought she'd abandoned for the duration of her pregnancy, had already set in. Although three quarters of the patrons at the Cheer would be in flannel, she wouldn't be caught on a date in it.

Okay, so she was going on a date. That didn't mean it had to lead anywhere.

THE CHRISTMAS CHEER encompassed one large, high-ceilinged room in an old brick building at the center of town. The walls were covered in old and new signage, photos of town events past and present, hunting and fishing trophies of the taxidermic sort and a large display of tarnished softball and bowling trophies. The bar extended along the longest wall, with a few tables at the center and rough wooden booths lining the perimeter beneath high, small, glass-block windows that allowed no light to brighten the barnlike space, even at high noon.

"I guess you've been here hundreds of times," Mike said as they slid into the last available booth.

Merry shook her head. "My late grandmother didn't approve of places that serve alcohol, so my mother rarely brought us here, even after they opened the grill. By the time I was old enough to come alone, I was off at college. But I used to stop by during the summer, usually with a boyfriend."

Mike nodded toward the bar, which was populated

with a lot of single males in flannel and jeans. "Which ones?"

"Did I date?" She colored as she surveyed the lineup before flicking a finger. "That one."

The guy she'd indicated looked like all the rest, although maybe a bit younger. Longish hair, a bit of a paunch, well-worn jeans. Rugged and outdoorsy.

"He's still interested," Mike said. "I saw him look you over when we arrived."

She grinned. "Forget it. He's been married for years to an old classmate of mine. They have three or four kids. The oldest is a teenager." She patted her midriff. "I'm getting a late start, especially in these parts. Almost everyone I used to know here got married in their early twenties."

"How did it feel, moving back home after being gone for so long?"

She thought about that. "Surreal, at first. It was weird how some people looked exactly the same and others I couldn't even recognize until they started talking. Usually those were the younger ones. My image of them was stuck in high school."

A young waitress came by, delivered ice water and took their orders from a menu that basically constituted a choice between fried fish or fried meat.

"The place is a little quiet," Merry commented.

"Early yet," the waitress said as she tucked her order pad into a short apron slung over her jeans.

"This is quiet?" Mike said over the music from the jukebox.

Merry nodded and took a sip of her water.

He settled in, giving up on his idea of having a private talk with her. He could bide his time. There were things that had to be said, as much as he dreaded being the cad who said them.

Waiting for the food, they made very little conversation. He looked around the tavern, noticing the looks that Merry got. She stood out, he believed, and so, it seemed, did everyone else. But not because she was pregnant, at least not to him.

It was her essence, the clarity and vivacity he'd noticed the first time he saw her. She had a different style, too, with her sleek hair and the sophisticated silver jewelry she wore with a black sweater, jeans and the leather boots with high chunky heels.

He could come back in ten years, twenty years, and she'd be the same. A rose among the thorns. A cardinal in the snow.

Ten, twenty years? Was that how long he needed?

MERRY DIPPED a French fry into ketchup and swirled it around. She'd had dumber ideas, but losing out on her last chance to spend real time with Mike was right up there among the dumbest. Not that she wanted to get into some big discussion about the future they both knew they didn't have. But just being easy with him, maybe hearing more of his Navy adventures, would have been nice. The other night at her house, he'd had her aching with laughter over a story about being dared to eat a dozen candied apples called cannonballs while at an academy affair. Then there'd been the crash and smash, a game which seemed to involve extreme quantities of beer and pilots jetting across long tables on their bellies.

Instead they were stuck at the Cheer, eating burgers and fries and waving every five minutes to overexcited female customers, most of whom tended to squeal and flutter when they saw that Merry was out with Mike.

"Post-Christmas stress relief," she called to him over the rising volume of chatter. "The women are letting their hair down."

He nodded and mouthed something. She leaned closer to make him out. "What about you?"

"You have to be a harried mother with a zillion responsibilities to get the full effect," she replied. "Check with me next year."

The last sentence was uttered during one of those momentary pockets of silence and she pressed her lips together, wishing she could take back the words. She'd made a promise to herself not to bring up the future at all. Not tomorrow, not next year, not ten years from now. She knew a skittish man when she shared a plate of fries with him.

Except *skittish* wasn't supposed to be a description that fit Mike. He was too solid to be skittish. He wasn't resistant anymore, either, after the past night. But what else was there?

Not unstable, or volatile, or fickle.

He was the opposite of those.

Unwilling, she decided. That was it.

She touched her belly. Who could blame him? Shock and reluctance had been her first reactions when she'd learned about the baby. After years of reliable birth control, having a condom fail during her last time with Greg had seemed like a cruel cosmic joke.

Until her mind had adjusted, she'd been pretty darn skittish herself.

"I'll do that," Mike said. She must have looked confused, because he added, with a lackadaisical shrug, "Check with you."

Next year.

She nodded and smiled.

Suddenly he gripped her hand. "Let's get out of here. I can't stand this noise."

He threw a couple of bills on the table and helped her into her coat. His own still had a few streaks of pitch on the front. She frowned over the stains, thinking of him a few days from now, finding a dry cleaner, having the last remnants of Christmas removed from his tidy life.

"Is there anywhere else you want to go?" Mike asked once they were in the car he'd borrowed from Grace, the rental having been returned the day after their arrival.

Merry held her hands by the heater vents. "No, just home."

But he didn't bring her straight there. He took a turn around the town first, looking at the Christmas lights and decorations. "I like this," he said, driving slowly back toward the highway that ran through the center of town. "The small-town Christmas experience."

"We must seem awfully quaint."

"Not awfully. Enjoyably."

"A nice place to visit, but you wouldn't want to live here?" she said, trying to sound lighter than she felt.

"Probably not, no."

That was veering too close to talk of the future. Merry grabbed at distraction. "Look, Oliver's car is parked outside Jackie's. I hope they're not only talking murder."

"Murder?" came Mike's startled query.

"Oliver's working on a new book, a murder mystery."

"Ah." Mike stopped at the corner, the turn indicator ticking. "Don't they seem like an odd couple to you?"

"Opposites attract."

The road was clear, but he didn't pull out. He was watching Merry's profile, which was all that she gave him, too self-conscious to let him see the feelings that must show in her face.

"You and I," he said. "We're not opposites."

"No, we're a lot alike. First children, high expectations, take our responsibilities very seriously, look out for…" She faltered. Every word out of her mouth carried too much weight.

He drove onto the highway, heading east toward the tree farm. A mile passed before he spoke. "I've been thinking. We don't have to say goodbye tomorrow and never be in contact again, do we? We can call, we can write. Even after I'm deployed again, this doesn't have to be the end."

The offer lit her up inside, but she steeled herself against it. "That sounds reasonable, in theory. But why drag it out?"

"It?"

"The inevitable."

Mike's hands tightened on the steering wheel. "So now it's inevitable that we split. Gosh, thanks for telling me."

"You told me, every time the subject came up. And that's fine. Let's not renege on that now, just because you're having a few sentimental regrets."

He glanced at her. "You're that unemotional?"

"Are you kidding?" Her laugh was shaky. Revealing. She covered her mouth with her mittened hand. "I'm trying to hold on to my dignity, here." She blinked hard. "If you want a blubbering, emotional basket case who'll beg you not to leave, you're with the wrong woman."

"You know that's not what I want. But…" He inhaled. "It might help if I had some hint from you that you're feeling as torn up about this as me."

Of course I am, she wanted to blurt. She was raw. Aching. One heart-wrenching sob away from the emotional basket case she stubbornly refused to become.

She held on to the arm rest as Mike turned off the highway, roaring past the tree farm onto the country lane that led to her cottage. Powdery snow sprayed from the tires.

He parked, but didn't turn off the engine.

This is it, Merry told herself. *We're done.*

"We can write," she said. She was desperate. Any contact at all, even if it only dragged out her pain, seemed preferable to walking away from him without a single hope to cling to.

"I want to hear about the baby." His voice was filled with caring, perhaps even love, whether or not he knew it. "You have to send pictures."

"Of the whale stage? Ha, ha." But she smiled.

"I never asked you if you've thought about names."

"Not too much, yet. But I know I'm staying away from anything Christmas-themed. No Joy, Herald, Kringle or Holly for me."

"I don't know. Kringle York has a certain ring to it."

"Yeah, a toilet bowl ring." She made a flushing motion. "Whoosh."

They laughed, as though the comment was high humor.

Mike's next question sucked every bit of oxygen out of the air. "*Will* the baby be a York?"

She held her breath. "Yes, of course."

"What if the father comes back into your life? That could happen. Some men need time, but eventually they get their heads straight and try to do what's right."

A silence lengthened, broken only by the hum of the engine. Merry stared straight ahead at the headlights reflecting off the snow banked against the front of her house. She was struggling for words, uncertain whether or not Mike hoped there'd be a man to step into the spot he was going to vacate.

At last she spoke. "You know the father is Greg, don't you?"

He pushed his arms straight against the wheel. "I figured. From what you said."

"Believe it. He's never going to be the father of my baby. I made an agreement with him. I won't ask for child support in return for him signing away all future claims of fatherhood. There'll be no custody fights, no shared visitation. Not in a year, not in ten years. He has no interest."

"The man's a fool."

"No, he's smart enough to know his limitations. He told me all along that he wasn't interested in marriage or children. I was the fool—the one who didn't recognize what I really wanted until my family needed me." She sighed. "And then when I found I was pregnant, I had to decide whether or not I could do this on my own. I knew it would be difficult, but the baby seemed worth the trouble. More than worth it."

"You're a strong woman."

"Sometimes I believe that, and other days, especially when I think about the actual logistics of caring for an infant, well… I'm lucky to have friends and family close by."

"But no father."

"No father."

Mike cleared his throat. "If I could, if I was in a position to help you out…"

"Don't."

"You know I would."

After a hesitation, she leaned over and kissed his cheek. "Thank you. You've given me hope, you know. I'd been feeling so alone, even surrounded by family, and having you come in to my life and make me feel attractive again, like a woman instead of only a pregnancy, that was…really nice."

She sat back. "I know now that there will come a day when a man does enter my life—at the right time. And he'll fall in love with my child, too, and we'll be happy."

The only man she could picture in such a scenario was Mike, but admitting that would be pressuring him, so she pushed off the ideal scenario of her dreams into a hazy, greeting-card future.

"Someday," she said with a sigh.

His expression was not cooperative. In fact, he looked like a man who'd been drubbed about the head by a boxing kangaroo.

She didn't want to stick around and see him struggle for words to explain how sorry he was that he couldn't be her knight in shining armor.

Before he said another word, she gave his arm a quick squeeze, babbled something about him not needing to walk her to the door and bolted from the car faster than most pregnant women were capable.

They could say goodbye tomorrow.

THE TRIP TO THE AIRPORT was not a sentimental journey of lovers parting amid a backdrop of romance and drama.

There was drama, with Skip and Georgie bickering the entire way, responding fractiously to the tension in the air. There was even romance, since Nicky had tied one last sprig of mistletoe to the rearview mirror. He and Shannon sneaked in kisses whenever they could.

Mike and Merry sat in the back of the van, completely silent, bordering on morose. After a while, he picked up her hand and held it until they reached the terminal. The night before, he'd had so many arguments and explanations ready to go, but she'd trumped every one before he even began. Now, he realized that words couldn't help him. Only actions mattered.

And he was leaving. That said it all.

They checked in at the airline counter. Soon the first boarding call was announced. Nicky's family came together in a huddle. The boys were big-eyed and solemn. Shannon was stoic. Nicky looked as crushed as Mike felt.

He pulled Merry aside. "Well, this is it."

She hugged him without hesitation. "Be safe."

He held her tightly, brushing his face against her hair for the last time. "You, too."

Suddenly she took him by the face, her palms pressed hard to his cheeks. "I'm glad we made love," she said fiercely, almost nose-to-nose. "I'll never regret that."

He kissed her, but the kiss was mournful, salted by the teary gasp that rose in her throat. "The only thing I regret is going away," he whispered. Their harsh breaths intermingled. "I love you, Merry. I'd stay if I could."

A broken sob buckled her. They clung together for as long as they could, until the final boarding call could not be ignored. Mike and Nicky looked at each other and found strength that enabled them to turn and walk away.

The airport was a small one, and after going through security they walked directly out of the terminal to the steps positioned at the door of the small propeller plane. Before boarding, they looked back and waved. Shannon was a trouper and she had Nicky's sons positioned at the row of windows in the waiting area. Their faces pressed to the glass as they waved.

Merry was nowhere to be seen. Mike was forced to depart without one final look at her. If his heart hadn't already cracked in two, that alone would have done it.

CHAPTER THIRTEEN

Meredith York
Christmas, MI
27 Dec
Dear Merry:

I'm writing from the plane, somewhere over Missouri, or maybe Kansas. One of those flat, square states. No snow, only clouds. Your brother is listening to his iPod and I'm staring out the window, trying to think of what to write.

I wish I knew. About what I said. Did I shock you? Make you happy? Cause you more grief? First, there was too much time to talk, and then there wasn't enough. I had planned out what to say, but I forgot all of it in those last few minutes and spoke on instinct. Now I wonder if that was a mistake.

But it was true. I love you. I don't know what that means, or even if it's something you wanted to hear. I'm not even sure if it changes anything between us, because I'm not free to do what I might want, and not even absolutely sure what that is.

But my concerns aren't important. You are.

What do you want? I hope I can find a way to give it to you.

Yours,

Mike

December 27

Dearest Michael,

I'm writing this only a few hours after you left Christmas. On the way home from the airport, Shannon and I tried to cheer the boys up by taking them to lunch and a video arcade, but I don't think we were particularly success-ful. On the drive home, all that the boys wanted to talk about was their Dad and Uncle Mike and how you were going back to fly jets in the war. Poor Shannon. She says that she never gets used to these separations, and that each time is as difficult as the last. Military life isn't easy, which of course you already know, but I didn't. Not so completely as I do now.

If what I'm feeling is one tenth of what Shan-non does, I can't understand how she survives.

Anyway, I'm back home now, curled up on the

couch with music playing and the snow drifting down. I realize that this isn't a very cheery letter, but I doubt that I'll send it, anyway, so I might as well write whatever I want.

What I want is to know if you really meant it when you said you loved me. Could that be possible when you were resisting so hard, or was it just one of those spur-of-the-moment things a person blurts out in an emotional moment? The more I think about it, the less real it seems. Maybe I dreamed it, because it was exactly what I wanted to hear, but never dared think.

But if it was a dream, I would have answered.

I would have said I love you, I love you, I love you...

But I can only say that to myself. Which means I definitely won't be mailing this letter.

Lt. Cdr. Michael Kavanaugh
San Diego, CA
December 31
Dear Michael,

Thank you for the letter! You must have mailed it as soon as you landed, because I didn't have long to wait to hear from you. Although there are times that even three days feels like forever. I will send you an e-mail next time, but I wanted your first letter from me to be an actual letter.

Shannon and the boys are doing well, after a few days of adjustment to missing their dad again. Kids bounce back fast.

And me. I'm the same—and totally different.

You asked what I want. I wish there was an easy answer.

But maybe there is, if I dare to write it.

I want a healthy baby, first of all. And then, if I could have anything in the world, it would be you. I would want you, you loving me and me loving you and both of us loving this baby.

Whew. That wasn't so difficult after all, and much easier to say on paper than in person. I'm not sure if I can send this letter, either, although I'll try.

I don't know what this means to us, being so far apart. Maybe it's like those New Year's Eve wishes that you write on a piece of paper and toss into the fire, hoping that some magical midnight wind will catch them as they burn away into nothing and turn them into truth.

So this is my wish, on a cold New Year's Eve. Don't take it too seriously, not yet. Let's wait and see if there's any magic in the air.

Love,

Merry

To: Meredith_York@YorkTreeFarm.com
From: Kavanm@cvn78.navy.mil
Subject: Happy New(s) Year
Don't know if you've gotten my letter yet, but things are happening fast here and I don't have time to wait for an answer. It looks like Nick and I will be shipping out sooner than expected. More details to follow.
In the meantime, Happy New Year to all of you in Christmas. Keep warm.
Mike

To: Kavanm@cvn78.navy.mil
From: Meredith_York@YorkTreeFarm.com
Subject: re: Happy New(s) Year
Dear Mike: I know you're busy preparing to leave, so I won't go on too long. Naturally, your news came as a shock. Shannon wasn't expecting a deployment so soon. We are doing as well as can be expected, and ready to offer any support that we can.
I did receive your letter and assume that by now you got mine. I feel sort of embarrassed about that, but put what I wrote down to a sentimental New Year's Eve moment. Please keep your mind on the job and don't worry about us at home.

I'll keep warm if you promise to stay safe.
Cheers,
Merry

> Meredith York
> Christmas, MI
> 11 Feb

Dear Merry:

Sorry I've been slow to write a real letter again. E-mail is not the same, and to be honest, it's taken me a while to figure out what I wanted to write. For one thing, I can't begin to compare to your eloquence. Pilots are dashing and romantic only in the movies.

I don't want to backpedal, either. But maybe we got carried away. I'm not taking back anything I said. I'm just worrying about you being alone and fretting too much about me. That's not good for you or the baby. If anything happens to me, I don't want you to be so devastated that you can't—

Scratch that. There's no imminent danger. I'm safe and always careful. I'll be all right, and so will Nicky. You know I can't make promises that would be unrealistic and out of my control, but I will do everything within my power to come back to Christmas someday. I want to meet your baby.

Love,
Mike

To: Kavanm@cvn78.navy.mil
From: Meredith_York@YorkTreeFarm.com
Subject: not worrying
Hello, Mike: Don't worry about me worrying. Even with the business shut down until spring, I'm finding plenty to do to keep me occupied. I have everything set up on the computer system now, and I work from home in splendid comfort. Which is lucky, because now that I'm more than seven months gone, I'm really feeling the effects of pregnancy. The baby kicks like a Rockette!
Hugs and kisses,
Merry & the lil' showgirl

To: Meredith_York@YorkTreeFarm.com
From: Kavanm@cvn78.navy.mil
Subject: Entertain Me
Mer: With all the talk about worry and war, the reality is that you wouldn't believe how boring life

aboard ship can be. Now and then we get a couple of hours of action, but mostly it's nothing but briefings and endless hours of hanging out in the squadron's ready room. So I think about you a lot. Nicky said that Shannon wrote you're a whale now. I never think of you as a whale, and I'm not sure that I want to, but send pics, if you dare.

Love, Mike

P.S. Just kidding about the whale. I know you're beautiful.

To: Kavanm@cvn78.navy.mil
From: Meredith_York@YorkTreeFarm.com
Subject: You asked for it!

Dear Foolish Man: Attached are a couple of jpegs of me in all my glory. I don't think of myself as a whale. I think of myself as a Rose Parade float. Especially since my mother got sick of seeing me in baggy, men's flannel shirts. She went out maternity shopping without me and brought back the most froufrou, ruffly getups you can imagine. She was so pleased with herself. How could I say I hated them? I put them on when I know she'll be over, which is pretty much every day now that it's eight months and counting.

Time flies, even when there are days that seem to last forever and nights that—well, I won't get into the nights. Suffice to say that sometimes I feel restless…and worried, sorry. But enough of that. I promised myself to only write cheery news to keep you entertained.

We're expecting the usual St. Patrick's Day snowstorm, but the snow will be melting soon enough. Already there are days with spring in the air. I can even see patches of bare ground! Hmm, what else is going on? My father has been harassing Jeff, imparting his tree-trimming wisdom. I'm afraid I'm to blame for that, tee hee. Shannon and Jackie came over and helped me fix up the baby nook—it's too small to be a room. We painted it a pretty shade of gender-neutral green. I'm still fairly sure that I'm having a girl, but I think she'll be a nature girl who loves green. Jackie is "dating" Oliver, although thus far their dates seem to consist of her making him dinner and "running into" him when he goes for a walk, which she manages to do almost every day. Noelle swears she aced her midterms. Skip and Georgie always ask after you. They grow by leaps and bounds, and so does Kathlyn, whose burbles are beginning to sound like words, if you speak Babaweewee.

And that's the news here. Feels like I'm in a holding pattern, waiting for the baby, waiting for you…

All our love,

Merry & Rocky

To: Meredith_York@YorkTreeFarm.com
From: Kavanm@cvn78.navy.mil
Subject: re: You asked for it!

I knew that you would be beautiful. I wish I was there to hold you, and take care of you when the baby comes, instead of stuck out here in the middle of the Persian Gulf. A couple of the squad's biggest jokers saw your pictures when I opened my e-mail, so now my new nickname is Daddy 'Merica instead of Cap'n America. I only tell you this because Nicky thinks it's hilarious and will spill the beans to Shannon anyway. What do you think? Will I ever live up to the name?

Yours,

Just Mike

To: Kavanm@cvn78.navy.mil
From: Meredith_York@YorkTreeFarm.com
Subject: Re: re: You asked for it!

Daddy 'Merica? Does that make me Mama 'Merica? Not sure if I can handle that one, since the task of taking care of just one tiny baby grows increasingly daunting. You, however, are the kind of man who's capable of any task put before you, including fathering an entire country. I've always seen you as the George Washington type.

I'm teasing, naturally. I don't know if your question

was serious, but if it was, I want you to know that I'm certain that if you tried, you would be the world's best dad. Or maybe have to wrestle Nicky for the trophy.

Mer(ica)

P.S. Speaking of names, what do you think of Alexandra? Or maybe Elisabeth. Matthew, if it's a boy.

To: Meredith_York@YorkTreeFarm.com
From: Kavanm@cvn78.navy.mil
Subject: Names
What happened to Rocky? I liked Rocky. :-D

To: Kavanm@cvn78.navy.mil
From: Meredith_York@YorkTreeFarm.com
Subject: re: Names
Rocky! You can't be serious. Go fly a jet and defend our country, and leave the important stuff like baby names to the brain trust at home. :-b
M.

To: Meredith_York@YorkTreeFarm.com
From: Kavanm@cvn78.navy.mil
Subject: Flying
Dear Merry: It's early morning on the ocean and I'm thinking about you again. My mind has no

discipline when I'm coming off the high of a flight. We practiced night landings tonight. I don't think I ever told you about those and maybe I shouldn't now, either, but I need someone to talk to besides Nick.

There's nothing like a night landing. You're flying through the black nothingness, putting all your trust in your instruments and what seems like the miracle of catching a wire, especially when there are only the amber lights below, and a flight deck that looks the size of a postage stamp. Then your adrenaline is pumping and sparks are flying and you feel the tailhook catch and you thank God for one more successful trap and for another shot at being the man you know you can be.

I can be that man for you, Merry. Let me try. Sometimes it still scares the stuffing out of me, the thought of being responsible for other human beings on the most personal level. And other times I think I'm an idiot for ever hesitating. Look at Ripper. He's the Blue Knights' biggest horse's ass, pardon my French, and he has a wife and three little kids who think he's a hero.

I don't want to be a hero. I just want to be there with you and Rocky and know that nothing bad will ever happen to any of us. And that's the catch, isn't it?

Love,

Mike

Lt. Cdr. Michael Kavanaugh
USS Jefferson
April 17
Dear Mike,

It was wonderful, talking to you on the phone. I can't seem to remember anything that I said, and not much of what you said, either. I would blame the drugs, but I had the minimum, so I suppose it was the female equivalent of your fighter pilot's high. My mind was racing. I was exhausted and exhilarated and just plain over the moon all at once.

Elisabeth is here! She's here! Ten fingers, ten toes and all other parts accounted for, too.

I remember that you asked me what she looks like, but I still can't say. She's small and red and wrinkled and so beautiful it makes my heart ache just to look at her. Or maybe that's only my other lingering pains, which frankly are nowhere near as bad as the ones I was supposed to forget about the moment my baby arrived—which is such a lie, by the way—but still, bad enough to make me say ouch a hundred times a day. Be glad you missed all that. Seventeen hours of labor? Who ever thought that would be a good idea?

Like you, I wish so badly that you could meet Elisabeth. But soon, I pray. I know you can't say when and Shannon keeps reminding me not to pin my hopes on the news reports, but I confess I do all the same. Purely selfish reasons—I want you here. Elisabeth wants you. Perhaps that's even why she came a couple of weeks early, to hurry you along.

So, anyway. I'm scribbling this from my bed at home. My mother slept on the couch last night, our first at home, and I was grateful to have her. Babies are such demanding creatures. I had thought that being nine months pregnant was tough, but that was a breeze compared to this, and we've barely begun! Shannon says that the first year is the hardest, and that I should expect to be a sleepwalking zombie through most of it. My dad is secretly thrilled. Openly joyous about the baby, of course—even though her name isn't Angel or Holly—but also giddy at the prospect of taking over the management of the business again, at least through the summer. Once in a while I cringe to think of what he'll do to my orderly spreadsheets and files, but for the most part I can't bring myself to care. When I do get back my old enthusiasm, Jeff has promised to be my double agent and fill me in on what I've missed. He's turned out to be a real gem.

Did I mention that Noelle has decided to come home for the summer instead of taking the internship she was offered downstate? I don't know what's going on with that girl, but I intend to have a stern talk with her about making a choice and sticking to it. If my brain hasn't gone completely to mama mush by then.

Well, about now, you're probably thinking that it has. I'm rambling, and oh, boy, there goes Elisabeth, crying again, so I'll put a stamp on this letter and call it good.

Next time, I'll be more coherent. Or not. Who knows?

Much love,

Merry

To: ShannonY@Yoopertalk.net
From: Kavanm@cvn78.navy.mil
Subject: Thanks

Hi, Shannon: Thanks for e-mailing the pics. I understand about Merry feeling besieged. You're right, Elisabeth is the cutest blond baby ever. Merry looks very happy, but tired. How is she? I've sent e-mails, but she rarely writes back more than a line or two. Is she doing okay, taking care of the baby on her own? Does she ever mention me?

Say hi to your kids from Uncle Mike.

Mike

To: Kavanm@cvn78.navy.mil
From: ShannonY@Yoopertalk.net
Subject: re: Thanks

Oh, Mike. Try not to fret about Merry and the baby. I know it's not easy being so far away, but you've really got to trust me. Merry can survive without you. Even without me! Maybe not Grace, LOL. Elisabeth is thriving and Merry is, too. Yes, she talks about you sometimes. Maybe not as much as she used to, because motherhood takes up all her time. That's how it is with an infant. It doesn't mean she's stopped loving you or anything crazy like that, if that's what you're thinking. Ask Nicky. He'll tell you how absorbing it is, being a new parent. I don't think we spent five minutes alone together during Skip's first year.

Hugs and kisses,

Shannon

P.S. Hurry home and see for yourself, Daddy 'Merica!!!

To: Kavanm@cvn78.navy.mil
From: Meredith_York@YorkTreeFarm.com
Subject: checking in

Dear Mike: Sorry about my recent brevities. Life with Elisabeth has been a challenge, but I think she's finally over her colic. I was able to get four hours of uninterrupted sleep last night. Pure bliss. I seem to have no time to open a newspaper or turn on the TV these days, but Shannon has been keeping me informed on developments overseas. We continue to hope and pray that you will be sent home very soon. And I've been thinking a lot about something you wrote a while ago. When you said you couldn't stand for anything bad to happen to us.

I don't know that I really understood what you meant until I had Elisabeth. Now it's crystal clear. I would fight like a tiger to protect her, and I can't even bring myself to imagine her enduring the smallest injury, let alone anything worse. No wonder the sorrow you've felt over losing your father has been debilitating enough to make you avoid future commitments.

At the same time, when you love someone, what choice do you have? Not loving them won't keep them safe. It won't even keep you safe.

Life is scary, isn't it? But it's also too beautiful to avoid. My heart clashes over this every time I look at Elisabeth in her crib, but then she opens her big blue eyes—yes, they're still blue—and smiles at me—Mom says it's gas, but I say it's a smile—and somehow I forget the fear and worry and concentrate on the here and now.

Lots of love and kisses, with more to give when you return,

Merry

29 May
Dear Dad:

It's been a long time. There are too many days that I forget what you sounded like, even what you looked like. For a while after the accident, I tried to keep you alive by talking about you a lot, but that was too hard on Mom and so I learned to hold you quietly in my heart instead. Now I think that maybe I held on to you too tightly—at least, some form of you. The dad I remember when I think of the real you wouldn't have wanted me to hurt for so long. You wouldn't have blamed me the way I blamed myself. Not a chance. You would have said to let go, to get over it. To live my life without regrets.

So that's what I'm trying to do now, even if it's coming quite a few years late. But not too late. Never too late.

I've fallen in love, Dad. Her name is Merry, short for Meredith. You would have liked her, especially because she could have held her own against you, hiking or fishing or golfing. She's damn smart, too, and funny and caring. She's everything to me.

Everything. And that makes me more afraid than any pilot should ever admit. Because even though I've learned to compartmentalize the risks of the job, I can't seem to do that with Merry.

She's everything. If I lost her the way I lost you…

But that's not what I meant to write to you, Dad. I meant to say, for the last time, that I'm sorry.

And goodbye.

Mike

To: Meredith_York@YorkTreeFarm.com
From: Kavanm@cvn78.navy.mil
Subject: Yes!
Merry: I'm coming home to Christmas.
Mike

CHAPTER FOURTEEN

AS SOON AS MERRY LEFT the table to go to the ladies' room, Shannon, Noelle and Jackie put their heads together. "Do you think she knows?" Shannon said, popping high like a gopher to look after Merry before ducking back down.

"Not a thing." Noelle eased lower in her chair. They were at the Matterhorn Inn, ensconced at a table under the ram's head, having a "just us girls" lunch sans children. It was Merry's first time away from her baby for any significant amount of time. Grace was babysitting Elisabeth and Kathlyn. "The last time she talked to Mike was five days ago, in San Diego. She still believes he's stuck there for another month."

"I think she suspects," Jackie said. "Female intuition."

Noelle scoffed. "If she has an inkling, it's because you two keeping smiling like the cat who swallowed the cardinal."

Shannon frowned. "You mean the canary. The cat swallowed a canary."

"Whatever." Noelle waved airily while speaking out of the side of her mouth. "Look sharp, ladies. She's coming back."

"Hey, you," Shannon said when Merry seated herself, cell phone in hand. "Aha. You called home. So let's hear it. Were Elisabeth and Kathlyn surviving without us?"

Merry made a wry smile as she tucked the cell into her purse. "Kathlyn was getting a pony ride on Grandpa's knee and Elisabeth was sleeping. I guess it's official—I'm one of those nauseating mothers who acts like her child is made of Ming china."

"Everyone is, the first time anyway," Shannon said. "You'll get over it."

Jackie flipped over a curl of lacy frisée and stared into her salad suspiciously. "I wasn't like that. The first time I got Lunkhead One to watch the baby alone, I was outta there like a shot. He was the one who kept calling. He couldn't find the Pampers, he couldn't find his earplugs, he thought that Jimmy looked too purple."

"Purple?" Merry was alarmed. She'd never considered that Elisabeth might turn colors.

"From crying." Jackie shrugged. "I told Lunkhead to pick him up. The idiot." She stabbed a cucumber slice on the tines of her fork and lifted it in a salute. "Those were the days. Thank God they're over."

Noelle yawned behind her hand. "All this baby talk is putting me to sleep. Can we change the subject?"

"To what? Men?" Merry exchanged an amused look with Shannon. "I suppose we have to talk about Jeff."

Noelle blushed and squirmed, then glanced around the busy restaurant with narrowed eyes, in case other diners had noticed her atypical reaction. "What do you mean?"

"Isn't it obvious?" Shannon wagged her shoulders. "You're in lo-ove."

"So? I've always loved Jeff."

"But right now you're in love." Merry wasn't certain how long it would last, but she'd been enjoying watching Jeff and Noelle act like sweethearts again, after coming within a millimeter of splitting up at Christmas. Noelle had apparently decided that she didn't like being a complete free agent as much as she'd imagined, because she'd returned in April with her sights reset on Jeff. They'd been lovey-dovey ever since. Two months without a fight—a new record for them.

"You two are adorable," Shannon said.

Jackie and Noelle looked at each other. One wrinkled her nose. The other rolled her eyes.

Merry pounced. "Don't put on that face, Jackie Marshak. You're as much in love as the rest of us."

"I don't do love," Jackie insisted. "At least, not the mushy kind. That's for novels. In real life, women like me get Lunkhead One and Lunkhead Two."

They were accustomed to Jackie's acerbity, so

Shannon only smiled. "Sounds like that makes Oliver, Lunkhead Three."

Jackie pierced a caper and held it aloft. "What's this? I shoulda ordered a burger."

"Oliver's no lunkhead," Merry said. "He's just shy."

"The glaciers are melting faster," Jackie griped.

Noelle flipped her hair over her bare shoulder. The weather was warm enough that she'd broken out her tanks, halter tops and Daisy Duke shorts, making the men of Christmas extremely happy. "Vamp him."

Merry pooh-poohed her sister. "That's your solution for everything."

"Well, it works."

"Not for Jackie."

Jackie peered from beneath her curly black bangs. "Why not Jackie? I can be sexy. I just have to remember to shave my legs first."

The women laughed and returned to their food. Merry had ordered broiled fish because she was trying to lose her baby weight, but she snitched several of Noelle's onion rings, bemoaning her weak willpower each time. "I shouldn't be eating this. I need to lose fifteen pounds before I see Mike again. He's never seen me trim. Of course, he never saw me huge, either, except in a couple of photos."

The other three exchanged furtive glances.

"What?" Merry said. "Do I sound narcissistic? I

know—" She stopped and took a breath. Thinking about Mike, back in the country safe and sound, made her heart lodge in her throat and beat like the wings of a caged bird. "I know there are more important considerations." Just getting to see him again would be enough.

Shannon started to jabber. "Fifteen pounds isn't bad at all. I gained almost fifty total, with Kathlyn. Nicky was away at sea and Mom stuffed me with home-cooking. I'm lucky I didn't gain seventy-five. Plus, it gets worse with each baby. You gain more and lose less. Your hips spread, too, and let's not even talk about what happens to your boobs."

Jackie cackled. "Look at Noelle's face. For that matter, look at Merry's."

She'd screwed up her features, trying to figure out the curious tension at the table. "What's going on?"

"Nothing," Shannon answered, too fast.

"Have another onion ring," Noelle said.

Jackie hid her face behind a tall glass of lemonade.

"You're all keeping something from me, and I'm going to find out what." Merry nibbled on an asparagus spear. "I'll ask Mom. She can't keep a secret."

"You do that," Shannon said, apparently relieved.

Merry resisted the urge to call again and check on Elisabeth, even though she didn't think their surreptitiousness had anything to do with her baby. But there was something, she was certain.

Maybe even something big. Already she could feel the flutter in the back of her throat.

SHANNON DROVE MERRY back to the farmhouse to pick up her baby, chattering like a magpie the entire way.

Merry stayed quiet. Anticipation had quickened her senses. Her eyes darted across the familiar landscape, grown lush and verdant. They passed the tree farm, with its rows of trimmed evergreens. The swathes of daisies that had sprung up along the ditches nodded in the warm June breezes.

Nothing out of the ordinary. Merry told herself to stay calm. She was reading too much into a few secretive glances and jumpy reactions. But as they traveled down the shaded driveway toward the farmhouse, she leaned forward with anticipation, her hands clenched in her lap.

Seeing no strange vehicles or other signs of visitors, she sank back again with a sigh. She felt a little silly for letting her hopes leap too high.

Several weeks before, Shannon had made a quick trip to greet her husband when the aircraft carrier had docked in its homeport. Merry hadn't been ready to make that step. Writing back and forth with Mike had been wonderful and illuminating, but safe. Seeing him again face-to-face after so long was daunting, especially when she thought about the words they'd exchanged.

She believed that her feelings for him had only grown richer and deeper during their months apart, but she couldn't really be certain until they were together again. So much had happened to both of them in the meantime.

"Here we are," Shannon said brightly as she parked the minivan.

"For a minute, I thought…" Merry let her voice trail off. "Uh, never mind."

Shannon didn't question the comment. That in itself renewed Merry's curiosity. There was a secret.

A smiling Grace greeted them at the door. Her gaze bounced between their faces. "Did you have a good lunch?"

"Great," Shannon said.

"It was nice to get out." Merry moved past her mother, whose voice stopped her.

"Elisabeth's not here."

"She's not?" That was strange.

"Grandpa took her with him on his daily walk, about five minutes ago. He said he'd meet you at your house."

"He took her with him? He never does that."

"We strapped her into the baby carrier."

Merry hesitated. Suspicions buzzed. "We just drove past my house and we didn't see him, but okay."

"You can meet him there," Grace repeated.

"All right. I'll go now. Do you have the diaper bag?"

Her mother's eyes widened.

Shannon bolted. "I'll get it." She was back in seconds, thrusting the bag at Merry. "Here."

Merry strolled outside, despite the feeling that they were rushing her. Shannon followed closely behind. She reached out and straightened the collar of Merry's blouse. "You look pretty."

"No spit-up stains, anyway."

Shannon smiled. Shannon smiled a lot, but not always so hugely. "I'll see you later," she said, and fled indoors, closing the door before Merry was able to offer a goodbye.

Positively bursting with secrets, Merry thought.

She headed home, swinging the diaper bag and feeling a little bit like Cinderella. Bluebirds should have swooped out of the sky with ribbons for her hair.

Six months ago, she'd walked this way with Michael, right after their first kiss, and after he'd realized that she was pregnant. Now there was little Elisabeth. And there was, maybe, a whole lot more.

She was getting excited again.

By the time she reached the main road, she was almost jogging. A car drove by and she imagined what she looked like to the occupants—a thirtysomething woman, plump and panting, a red diaper bag bumping against her hip. Running where? Why?

Because she couldn't get Michael out of her head.

She stopped at the turn toward her house to catch

her breath. Her blouse had gapped across her breasts. She redid the button, smoothed herself out with shaky hands. One turn and the house would be within sight. Was she totally crazy for thinking that Mike might be waiting for her there?

She started forward. Too nervous to look, she closed her eyes as she rounded the bend, but only took a few steps before she stopped. A dozen meetings with Mike flipped past her mind's eye in an instant— him peering between the cereal boxes at her in the grocery store, sitting on the couch with her father between them, catching him with his shirt off upstairs, kissing beneath the mistletoe, kissing him on the couch…and in bed, kissing at the airport after he'd said that he loved her. She'd kicked herself a thousand times since then for being too overcome to respond. If he was here now, standing in front of her, she'd say it back to him, she was certain. She'd been waiting too long to blow the chance.

Her lids opened.

A shaft of sunlight struck her eyes. She shaded them, striding forward, suddenly confident that she was not being a hopelessly hopeful romantic.

A man moved out from beneath the roof overhanging her front steps. Her father? No. This was a tall man, lean and hard, with a memorable set of shoulders.

It was Mike, really, truly Mike. Startlingly handsome in his dress uniform of summer whites.

Merry gave a small cry and dropped the diaper bag. She was running, with no thought to how ruffled she looked or how hard she panted. Joy surged through her, a tiding of the greatest joy known to womankind this side of Christmas.

Mike ran, too. They crashed into each other with a *whump* that stole Merry's breath. Then she was in his arms. He was lifting her off her feet, swinging her around, and she was laughing and kissing him and nothing had ever felt more right and less uninhibited than those first few seconds of pure elation.

Mike put her down. She pulled back to look at him in the crisp white uniform and said, "Handsome!" with a gasp of a laugh.

He put his face against hers. "Beautiful."

"Am I dreaming?"

"Pinch me. I'm real."

He was real, all right. Her hands were all over him, settling at last on his face. His cap had been knocked to the back of his head and she tugged it lower before kissing him beneath the brim. Her heart was racing a mile a minute. "I can't believe you're here. Why didn't you tell me?"

"My leave came through at the last minute, so I decided to make a surprise visit. You really didn't know?"

"Shannon and the rest of them gave it away, sort of, but don't say I told you. I had almost convinced myself that I was wrong on the walk over, except I couldn't think of any other reason they'd act so secretive." She shuddered from the thrill. "Is Nicky here, too? What about Elisabeth?"

"Nicky's still on base, finishing up his paperwork. Elisabeth is over at your mother's. They sent you here on a ruse."

"Then you saw her?"

He nodded. "Beautiful. She looks like you."

Merry beamed, although she felt sure that he was exaggerating. "You can't really tell, with an infant."

"She has your eyes. And I think she got me to fall in love at first smile. Just like her mom."

Merry was already too flushed with excitement to turn any pinker, but Mike's words managed it. Her worries about reconnecting with him suddenly seemed inconsequential, even though there was a strange newness to their intimacy.

She pressed her lips against his jaw. "Welcome home, stranger."

"I'm no stranger. You know me." The low timbre of his voice gave her a delicious chill.

"Not in this uniform." She ran a hand across the starched white jacket, admiring its fit and the hard-earned insignia. His golden wings gleamed above the color bar. "You're a liar, by the way. You wrote that you're not a romantic, dashing hero, but here you are."

She kissed him once. "Dashing."

Twice. "Romantic."

A third time. "Very much a hero."

He smiled, touching his nose to hers. "We have a lot to talk about, you and me, but first we'd better go back to your parents' place and let them know the plan worked and you were suitably surprised."

"Yes. We can pick up Elisabeth."

"You mean Rocky."

"She's going to be called Beth."

"But what's her middle name?"

"It's not Stallone."

"Raquel," Mike said with a big grin. "I'm guessing you chose that for a reason."

"That was your fault. Yours and Shannon's and Nicky's. They'd already used Charles—Skip's real name—and Kathlyn Grace. So Rocky was all that I could think of when they asked me for the baby's middle name. My dad keeps mentioning how fond he was of the fur bikini that Raquel Welch wore in some B movie. I haven't explained."

Mike had chuckled through her breathless recitation. "Well, good. Rocky will be our private nickname."

Our. Things were happening so quickly, Merry felt as if the top of her head might blow off. Had she agreed to more than she remembered?

She licked her lips. "Our?"

"Our," he repeated, with the staunch air of a man who would not be swayed. "Rocky is our daughter."

"Are you certain?"

He nodded. "As far as I'm concerned, she never had any other father but me."

"You don't have to—"

"I want to. I always have. It just took me a while to get to a place where I could make the promise."

Merry hugged him around the waist. "Maybe we should slow down. You're taking my breath away."

Through the dapples of sunlight, Mike walked her to the front steps of her cottage and sat her down beside a glazed ceramic pot filled with dark purple salvia. The tall evergreens that surrounded the house made it shaded and private, even with the humming sound of cars passing on the nearby highway.

He sat beside her. "What do you want to know?"

"Um…" She gave a flustered laugh. "Everything? We've been apart for six months and a lot has happened."

"Rocky was born. We covered that."

"Oh?" She laughed again in defense, taken aback by his apparent single-mindedness. She'd known he was a man who stuck to his guns once he'd made up his mind. Did his certainty mean that he'd made up his mind about her? Perhaps it was a woman thing, but she had to know why before she made up her own.

"I wish I'd been here for that," he added softly.

"Hey, that's okay. You were sort of busy at the time."

"Next time."

"Oh, Lord. What does that mean?"

"It means that even though I'm staying in the Navy, I will be assigned to shore command for the next several years. I've been considering the option to work as an instructor at the Naval Academy in Annapolis. Have you ever been to Maryland?"

"Wha— Wait. This is huge news." She waved her hands in little circles. "Let me process."

He waited, regarding her so steadily that she began to feel the bird's wings in her throat again. She'd never been a nervous, fluttery person, but Michael made her feel that way all the time, at least inside. Outwardly, she was doing her best to remain calm.

She clasped her hands in her lap. "You've made up your mind, then. You're staying in the Navy for good?" She knew that aviators were required to make a long commitment after receiving their wings, but Nicky and Mike had fulfilled that requirement with their most recent sea tour.

For the first time, Mike hesitated. "I should have talked to you first."

"Well, we're not..." She couldn't finish the sentence.

"Close enough."

"It's your decision," she said. After all, she'd been making plenty of her own, on her own.

"I want it to be our decision."

"Oh." She linked her fingers. His gaze remained on

her face, but she couldn't look at him, not quite yet. "Ultimately, you have to do what's right for you."

He took her hands, pried them apart, enfolded them between his. "Except that I want it to be right for you, too. I know it's a lot to ask, but would you ever consider moving away from Christmas to be with me?"

She inhaled. They were surrounded by plant life, and still there wasn't enough oxygen to make up for him stealing her breath at every turn.

"Merry? What do you say?"

She nodded. "I believe that I would move for you. I'd never considered myself one of those 'wherever you go, I go,' women, but I am willing to compromise. And as much as I've enjoyed being home the past year and a half, I can move on without regret." She smiled, tilting her head to tap it against Mike's shoulder. "Maybe you've read between the lines of my letters. I've been setting things up so I can hand the family business back over to my father and Jeff."

"You're sure?"

"I want the business to thrive, but that can happen without me. Being a tree farmer was never the way I'd planned to spend the rest of my life." She chuckled. "I don't know what Noelle will say, though, when she realizes that she's the one who might be faced with living in Christmas for the foreseeable future."

"Her and Jeff?"

"Hot and heavy, for now. Mom is already talking wedding, and Dad has mentioned making Jeff a partner."

"Then that's settled."

"We'll see what Noelle does, but for my part, yes, it's pretty much settled."

"And what do you think of Maryland?"

"I could live there."

He smiled. "Great."

"Wait. I'm not necessarily the stay-at-home type, you know. Maybe for a while, but not forever. Before too long, I'll want to go back to my career. Can you handle that?"

"You bet."

"You're very certain. How come? A lot of guys like the convenience of having a—a—" She couldn't bring herself to say wife. Not yet. She wasn't shy, but this was an area where she was old-fashioned. Thus far, they'd done a fine job of talking around the crucial question, but sooner or later, he was going to have to lay it on the line.

"I grew up in a two-career family. It worked out fine." Mike's head dropped. His voice tightened. "We didn't start to fall apart as a family unit until after my father passed on."

She tapped him with her forehead, giving silent support. The tree branches rustled. "About that..." she whispered.

"I'm working on it."

"Working on it?"

"You wrote to me, more than a month ago it was, about how not loving someone won't keep them safe any more than loving them will, and that really resonated with me. I saw that because I didn't want to take any risks, I'd been closing myself off from all the good in life, as well as the bad. I decided it was time to change."

Her heart swelled. "I'm proud of you. That's a big step."

He grinned a bit sheepishly. "Only a step. I expected it to be simple, but I found out that I couldn't change overnight, just because I'd made up my mind to do it. But I'm getting there." He cleared his throat. "Most of all, I'd like to get there with you, Merry."

She nodded, too overwhelmed to speak.

"I hadn't exactly planned it this way, but…"

He swept off his hat. He dropped to one knee, still holding her hands in her lap. "I love you, Meredith York. Possibly from the first time I laid eyes on you, coming toward me out of the snowstorm, the only spot of color in a world of black and white."

He lifted her clasped hands and gave them a quick kiss. "I love you and I want to marry you. Will you take me as your husband and a father for Rocky? Will you be my wife?"

His absolute confidence infused her, even though

she believed that she'd made up her mind months ago and had only been in a holding pattern, waiting for his return.

"Yes," she said, and they went into each other's arms, sprawled in an ungainly but blissful embrace upon the steps.

"Hold on, hold on," she said, laughing as he planted big, sloppy, smacking kisses all over her face. "I've waited six months to say this, ever since the airport." He'd put his arms under her and scooped her part way into his lap, half on and half off the steps. She was jittery and tousled and she didn't care about anything except setting free the words that had been trapped too long inside her.

"I love you, Mike. I love you so much. And I know that Elisabeth will, too."

"Rocky," he said.

"All right, then. Rocky." She touched a fingertip to his lower lip. "You and me and Rocky."

Mike's eyes were alight with promise. "A brilliant flight crew, if ever there was."

"Brilliant," she agreed, as the clouds shifted and the trees stirred, allowing a beam of sunlight to pour over them. "Absolutely brilliant."

Brad shoved the truck into gear and drove to the bottom of the hill, where the road forked. Turn left, and he'd be home in five minutes. Turn right, and he was headed for Indian Rock.

He had no damn business going to Indian Rock.

He had nothing to say to Meg McKettrick, and if he never set eyes on the woman again, it would be two weeks too soon.

He turned right.

He couldn't have said why.

He just drove straight to the Dixie Dog Drive-In.

Back in the day, he and Meg used to meet at the Dixie Dog, by tacit agreement, when either of them had been away. It had been some kind of universe thing, purely intuitive.

Passing familiar landmarks, Brad told himself he ought to turn around. The old days were gone. Things had ended badly between him and Meg anyhow, and she wasn't going to be at the Dixie Dog.

He kept driving.

He rounded a bend, and there was the Dixie Dog. Its big neon sign, a giant hot dog, was all lit up and going through its corny sequence—first it was covered in red squiggles of light, meant to suggest ketchup, and then yellow, for mustard.

Brad pulled into one of the slots next to a speaker, rolled down the truck window and ordered.

A girl roller-skated out with the order about five minutes later.

When she wheeled up to the driver's window, smiling, her eyes went wide with recognition, and she dropped the tray with a clatter.

Silently Brad swore. Damn if he hadn't forgotten he was a famous country singer.

The girl, a skinny thing wearing too much eye makeup, immediately started to cry. "I'm sorry!" she sobbed, squatting to gather up the mess.

"It's okay," Brad answered quietly, leaning to look down at her, catching a glimpse of her plastic name tag. "It's okay, Mandy. No harm done."

"I'll get you another dog and a shake right away, Mr. O'Ballivan!"

"Mandy?"

She stared up at him pitifully, sniffling. Thanks to the copious tears, most of the goop on her eyes had slid south. "Yes?"

"When you go back inside, could you not mention seeing me?"

"But you're Brad O'Ballivan!"

"Yeah," he answered, suppressing a sigh. "I know."

She rolled a little closer. "You wouldn't happen to have a picture you could autograph for me, would you?"

"Not with me," Brad answered.

"You could sign this napkin, though," Mandy said. "It's only got a little chocolate on the corner."

Brad took the paper napkin and her order pen, and scrawled his name. Handed both items back through the window.

She turned and whizzed back toward the side entrance to the Dixie Dog.

Brad waited, marveling that he hadn't considered incidents like this one before he'd decided to come back home. In retrospect, it seemed shortsighted, to say the least, but the truth was, he'd expected to be—Brad O'Ballivan.

Presently Mandy skated back out again, and this time she managed to hold on to the tray.

"I didn't tell a soul!" she whispered. "But Heather and Darlene *both* asked me why my mascara was all smeared." Efficiently she hooked the tray onto the bottom edge of the window.

Brad extended payment, but Mandy shook her head.

"The boss said it's on the house, since I dumped your first order on the ground."

He smiled. "Okay, then. Thanks."

Mandy retreated, and Brad was just reaching for the food when a bright red Blazer whipped into the space beside his. The driver's door sprang open, crashing into the metal speaker, and somebody got out in a hurry.

Something quickened inside Brad.

And in the next moment Meg McKettrick was standing practically on his running board, her blue eyes blazing.

Brad grinned. "I guess you're not over me after all," he said.

Inside ROMANCE

Stay up-to-date on all your romance reading news!

Inside Romance is a FREE quarterly newsletter highlighting our upcoming series releases and promotions.

Visit
www.eHarlequin.com/InsideRomance
to sign up to receive our complimentary newsletter today!

REQUEST YOUR FREE BOOKS!
2 FREE NOVELS PLUS 2 FREE GIFTS!

HARLEQUIN®

Super Romance®

Exciting, emotional, unexpected!

YES! Please send me 2 FREE Harlequin Superromance® novels and my 2 FREE gifts. After receiving them, if I don't wish to receive any more books, I can return the shipping statement marked "cancel." If I don't cancel, I will receive 6 brand-new novels every month and be billed just $4.69 per book in the U.S., or $5.24 per book in Canada, plus 25¢ shipping and handling per book and applicable taxes, if any*. That's a savings of close to 15% off the cover price! I understand that accepting the 2 free books and gifts places me under no obligation to buy anything. I can always return a shipment and cancel at any time. Even if I never buy another book from Harlequin, the two free books and gifts are mine to keep forever.

135 HDN EEX7   336 HDN EEYK

Name	(PLEASE PRINT)
Address	Apt.
City	State/Prov.	Zip/Postal Code

Signature (if under 18, a parent or guardian must sign)

Mail to the **Harlequin Reader Service**®:
IN U.S.A.: P.O. Box 1867, Buffalo, NY 14240-1867
IN CANADA: P.O. Box 609, Fort Erie, Ontario L2A 5X3

Not valid to current Harlequin Superromance subscribers.

Want to try two free books from another line?
Call 1-800-873-8635 or visit www.morefreebooks.com.

* Terms and prices subject to change without notice. NY residents add applicable sales tax. Canadian residents will be charged applicable provincial taxes and GST. This offer is limited to one order per household. All orders subject to approval. Credit or debit balances in a customer's account(s) may be offset by any other outstanding balance owed by or to the customer. Please allow 4 to 6 weeks for delivery.

Your Privacy: Harlequin is committed to protecting your privacy. Our Privacy Policy is available online at www.eHarlequin.com or upon request from the Reader Service. From time to time we make our lists of customers available to reputable firms who may have a product or service of interest to you. If you would prefer we not share your name and address, please check here. ☐

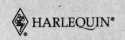

HARLEQUIN®

American ★ Romance®

Kate Merrill had grown up convinced
that the most attractive men were incapable
of ever settling down. Yet the harder she
resisted the superstar photographer
Tyler Nichols, the more persistent the
handsome world traveler became.
So by the time Christmas arrived, there
was only one wish on her holiday list—
that she was wrong!

LOOK FOR

THE CHRISTMAS DATE

BY

Michele Dunaway

**Available December
wherever you buy books**

COMING NEXT MONTH

#1458 GOING FOR BROKE • Linda Style
Texas Hold 'Em

Jake Chandler swore he'd never return to River Bluff, Texas, after being run out of town when he was eighteen, wrongfully accused of arson. But a funeral brings him back. And Rachel Diamonte, the witness to his supposed crime, just might be the woman who keeps him here. Because when it comes to love, the stakes are high....

#1459 LOOKING FOR SOPHIE • Roz Denny Fox

Garnet Patton's life hasn't been the same since her ex-husband abducted their five-year-old daughter and left Alaska. Then Julian Cavanaugh, a detective from Atlanta, comes to town, claiming he might have some new information. Will he be able to find her daughter…and will he be able to lead Garnet back to love?

#1460 BABY MAKES THREE • Molly O'Keefe
The Mitchells of Riverview Inn

Asking for his ex-wife's help is the last thing Gabe Mitchell wants to do. But he needs a chef, and Alice is the best. Working together proves their attraction is still strong. So is the issue that drove them apart. Is this their second chance...or will infertility destroy them again?

#1461 STRANGER IN A SMALL TOWN • Margaret Watson
A Little Secret

Kat is determined to adopt Regan, her best friend's child. Only one thing stands in her way—Seth Anderson. Seth has just learned he is Regan's father, and even though he's no family man, he wants to do right by the little girl. Especially once he realizes Kat is a suspect in the investigation he's conducting.

#1462 ONE MAN TO PROTECT THEM • Suzanne Cox

He says he can protect her and the children, but how can Jayden Miller possibly trust Luke Taylor—when the public defender is clearly working for some very nasty men? With no one else in Cypress Landing to turn to, Jayden is forced to put their lives in his hands....

#1463 DOCTOR IN HER HOUSE • Amy Knupp

When Katie Salinger came back to recuperate from her latest extreme-sport adventure, she didn't expect her dad to have her childhood home up for sale. The memories tied to it are all she has left of her mom. Worse: there's an offer…from the mysterious Dr. Noah Fletcher.

HSRCNM1107